M000207259

Speak for Me

DEBORAH ROGERS

Copyright Information

ISBN 978-0-473-52143-1
TITLE: Speak for Me
First worldwide publication 2020
Copyright © 2020 Deborah Rogers

All rights reserved in all media. No part of this book may be used
or reproduced without written permission, except in the case of brief
quotations embodied in critical articles and reviews.

The moral right of Deborah Rogers as the author of this work has
been asserted in accordance with the Copyright, Designs and Patents
Act 1988.

This is a work of fiction. Any resemblance to any actual persons,
living or dead, places, or events is entirely coincidental.

Published by Lawson Publishing (NZ).

For my sister, Sandra.

1

I'm going to be sick. I stare into the wide-open mouth of the toilet bowl and wait. Nothing happens. I don't have time for this. I've got work to do.

I sit back and try to gauge whether or not it's safe to return to my desk. It's difficult to tell. A few weeks back, I decided I was okay and then ended up vomiting in the breakout area by the lift. In a potted plant. A yucca, I think.

My co-workers used to come and check on me. There would be this soft rap on the bathroom door—Sally from reception or Mike the young prosecutor who sat in the desk next to mine or John Liber my boss. Hey, kiddo, how you doing in there? Everything okay? I'd call back I'm good, thank you, John, even though I wasn't. And they'd leave me alone again. Until I'd emerge sometime later, pink-faced and clammy and smelling of breath mints.

It's sweet, really. The way everyone cares.

I never knew pregnancy could be this bad. Six weeks until the baby comes and I'm still gripped by these sudden, overwhelming bouts of nausea. Originally, my obstetrician, Dr. Sandy Liu, said it was likely the nausea would go away in the first trimester. But it never did. In later check-ups, Sandy said that sometimes these things happen and no one knows why. That some women have easy pregnancies and others have hard ones. She said the baby was growing normally and that was all that mattered. Essentially, Sandy was telling me to suck it up and deal with it. So I did. For these past seven-plus months, I've learned to live with the nausea just as you might learn to live with an ingrown toenail that flares up in an occasional and inconvenient way.

And now there's this thing with my blood pressure. Awhile back I got dizzy and Ethan panicked and insisted I get checked out and now I have to wear this stupid heart rate monitor. I feel like a prisoner with this clunky black thing on my wrist—on home detention for the crime of being pregnant. It's like a Fitbit on steroids and looks more appropriate for a mega-endurance athlete than an expectant mother. The thing is super sensitive, too. I only have to cough and the monitor emits a frantic, piercing beep, which never fails to startle me. Pretty counterproductive as far as I'm concerned. But I wear it because it makes Ethan feel better.

Me being pregnant has definitely brought out his paternal side, that's for sure. He hovers around me like I'm made of glass. Oh, I know he tries his best to restrain himself, but I feel his eyes on me all the time, trying to anticipate my every need, readying himself to open a door or hand me a cushion when mostly I just wish he would leave me alone.

On the other hand, I have to admit there are undeniable benefits to having a personal butler—like getting a warm bath drawn for me every night, hour-long foot massages, and midnight convenience store runs for Little Debbie snack cakes and double cheese Doritos. But what I really want is to get back to normal. To have my body be my own again. And I honestly think I might scream if one more person offers me their seat.

I haven't told anybody, but I've wondered if the upset stomach and blood pressure issues are anxiety-related rather than baby-related. If my mind is up to its old tricks again. That dreadful obsessive-compulsive disorder which drove me to repeatedly check my windows and locks had all but vanished when Rex Hawkins was finally captured. But that didn't mean anxiety couldn't rear its ugly head in other ways, did it? Is it possible that I have some sort of internal fear I'm not processing consciously? Is my body trying to tell me that something is still broken inside my head?

Last Thursday I went to see Lorna about it. Nobody knows this. Not even Ethan. I felt compelled to go because every night for an entire week, I woke up at 3 a.m. thinking about Lorna's pretty gray-blue Persian rug. It had been well over a year since our last session. That had been a fun one because we'd celebrated the fact that I had not checked my windows and doors for six months by having an afternoon tea of gluten-free raspberry and white chocolate muffins courtesy of the bakery downstairs from her office. I remember eating and joking and casting looks around her office, feeling like I'd somehow graduated, that I would never return to this place, with its low-hanging, teal-trimmed curtains, comfy sofa with the stylish mauve cashmere throw, and canisters of Japanese lime loose-leaf tea sitting on the sideboard.

But the 3 a.m. Persian rug disruptions were like a prod in the chest. An awakening of sorts. I'd heard somewhere that if you wake up thinking of something at 3 a.m., pay attention because that's God trying to send you a message. So I went to see Lorna. If she was surprised to see me, she didn't show it. Her face was its usual study of calm, non-judgmental self-possession.

"How have you been?" she said, folding her hands into her lap.

I told her I might be experiencing symptoms of anxiety. I told her I'd been waking up thinking of her gray-blue Persian rug. I told her I could be getting messages from God.

"I see."

"I'm joking about the God thing," I said.

Perhaps you're internalizing things, she said. Internalizing what? I countered. I couldn't be happier about becoming a mother. Sure, it was a bit of a shock at first—Ethan and I had only been married for three months when I found out I was pregnant—but once I got used to the idea, I was overjoyed. Well, overjoyed might be pushing it. Excited and scared, because who knew what kind of mother I would make? Did I really have what it takes to bring up a child? But I wasn't alone, was I? I had Ethan.

"What else is going on in your life?" asked Lorna.

She gave me a look and we both knew who she was talking about. Rex Hawkins.

I glanced away. "It's got nothing to do with him. I'm a different person now."

"We all process anxiety in different ways, Amelia. Are you taking time for yourself, taking things easy, preparing for the birth?"

She fired questions at me and I felt defensive. Like I was being a bad mother already.

"It's difficult," I said. "With work."

"Work?"

"The plea deal interview is soon."

"Ah, I see."

The plea deal. The one where Rex Hawkins required that I, his one and only surviving victim, be there to record his confession.

"How do you feel about seeing him again?" she asked.

The image of me and Rex Hawkins sitting in a tiny room flashed before my eyes and my blood pressure monitor bleeped.

"What I feel is the need to close this thing before the baby comes. To make sure she grows up in a world where men like Rex Hawkins are behind bars for the rest of their lives. To make sure that the victims' families finally get some peace of mind about what happened to their sisters and daughters. To make sure someone speaks for them."

"That sounds like a lot of pressure."

I shifted my eyes away from hers. "I can't back out now. Besides, he won't talk to anyone else. There's no plea deal without me there. He insisted."

Lorna nodded. "You feel responsible."

"I've been given the responsibility whether I like it or not."

"You could say no, put you and your baby first."

I paused, feeling slightly hurt. "You're judging me."

"Is that how it feels?"

I reached for my cane and hoisted myself to my feet.

"You don't understand, Lorna."

"No?"

My cane wobbled under my grip as I turned to look at her.

"Coming here was a mistake."

She nodded. "Okay."

"I can deal with things myself."

"Okay."

I looked at her, exasperated. "Stop saying that."

I turned for the door and glimpsed myself in the large picture book window. It looked like I had a giant eight-pound beach ball in my stomach. I placed a hand on it, felt the slight tremor beneath my palm.

"We'll be fine," I said.

Lorna paused and looked at me with her calm brown eyes. "Amelia, I think you'll make a wonderful mother."

Now as I rise from my knees to flush the toilet, I think of what I said back there in Lorna's office. We'll be fine. I'll be fine. Everything will be fine. Before I managed to escape out the door, Lorna had urged me to see her weekly until things had "settled down." But I'm not that person anymore. I have gone through the eye of the needle. I can stand on my own two feet (albeit with the assistance of a cane). I can look that son-of-a-bitch in the eye and get him to tell me the truth about what he did to those other women. Those other women who, just like me, trusted a handsome stranger and made the biggest mistake of their lives.

I grab my cane from where it's resting in the corner of the cubicle. Now the time has arrived. Tomorrow I will be seated across from Rex Hawkins, two years to the day since I shot him in my apartment. I used to wish I had killed him. That dark, vengeful part of me wanted him to rot in the ground. That dark part of me also wanted it to be my bullet that put him there.

But he had lived and I realize now that it is better that way because this thing is bigger than just me and my desire for revenge. Others are relying on me to see that justice is done for their loved ones. I brush down my hair with my hand and reach for the bathroom door. Getting justice for the victims is exactly what I intend to do.

2

I spend the next two hours absorbed in the Rex Hawkins case files. Checking and rechecking the facts. I want to be prepared for tomorrow. It's my one and only shot to make sure he admits everything he's done. If he tries to be evasive or misleading or inconsistent, I want to be able to hold him to account, to point out his errors and lies and omissions. The only way I can do that is if I know the case inside and out. Every sad and disturbing detail. Every name and every face. Every rape and every murder. I need to know what he's done even better than he does. The families are relying on me. The victims, too.

I'm just about to review the location maps again when I notice a missed call from Ethan. I look at my watch and my heart drops. I was supposed to meet him at a property viewing twenty minutes ago.

I find myself hesitating. I should really go. And I should really go now. But there's still so much work to be done here. I lift the phone and punch in his number. My heart thumps as I wait for him to answer. I hang up. I can't let him down. Not again. That would be twice in a row. He deserves better than that so I gather up my things, shove my files and laptop into my satchel, shrug into my coat, and head out the door.

He's waiting on the steps of the brown brick triplex in Queens. He's in profile looking up at the steel blue sky shrouded in low-lying clouds. I feel a sudden surge of love. Such a handsome and giving man. Broad-shouldered with dark hair skimming his jacket collar and a faint scar above his top lip, he reminds me of an old-fashioned film star. A modern-day Jimmy Stewart or Burt Lancaster. Well-mannered and honorable. A man who could draw you in with his kind, warm eyes.

He smiles when he sees me and my cane clapping up the street toward him. When I reach him, he takes me in his arms.

"Hello, lovely."

"God, Ethan, I'm so sorry. I lost track of time."

He's kind enough not to mention that this isn't the first time. He doesn't need to. I'm well aware of how much I find myself apologizing these days.

"You're here now," he says.

My heart monitor bleeps. Ethan frowns but I head him off at the pass.

"I was rushing from the subway."

I see him fighting not to say something.

"I'm fine. Really, I am." I smile and clasp his arm in an effort to reassure him I'm not about to go into labor or drop dead in the street.

Just then the real estate agent drives up in his metallic blue Tesla. In three deft movements, he angles the vehicle into an extremely tight parking space wedged between a dirty white pickup and a vintage Porsche Carrera. He emerges impeccably dressed in a dark charcoal three-piece suit and brown-blond hair coiffed to perfection. He doesn't look a day over twenty-five.

"Thanks for the heads-up about running late," he says, extending a nicely moisturized hand first to me then to Ethan. "I'm Peter."

He gestures for us to follow him up the steps to the glossy black painted door and explains that he's normally

9

a commercial agent but is doing this viewing as a favor for a friend. New York is all about doing favors for friends. Peter opens the door with a key code and we follow him inside until we come to the first apartment on the lowest floor of the triplex.

"You guys know this listing needs work, right?" says Peter, before opening the door.

I shoot Ethan a look. He never said anything to me about work.

"Let's just check it out," whispers Ethan.

Peter unlocks the door, moving aside so Ethan and I can enter first, and we step into what is a relatively large foyer and kitchen. The area is well-lit with the last rays of sun streaming through the huge bay window, but the space has little else going for it. Floorboards are missing and there's a massive hole in the wall. Not to mention the fact that some vandal has spray-painted the word "Blight" on the far wall above the radiator.

"I see someone has started the renovations already," jokes Peter.

We wander into a living room with extraordinarily high ceilings then take the stairs up to the main bedroom, which is sunny and small. Again more absent floorboards, although this time the cause looks more like wood-rot than vandalism. There's also a water stain in the right-hand corner of the ceiling.

Next to the bedroom there's another small room, just big enough for a single bed and maybe a chest of drawers. What appears to be mold is growing up one side of the wall near the tiny window. I glance at Ethan, who looks entirely captivated by the house. It's oozing from his pores, how badly he wants a home. So badly, that even this dilapidated money-pit will do.

Peter looks down at the specs sheet. "Great area. Easy access to transportation, subways and crosstown buses to any location in the City. Guarantors allowed, pets allowed, and sublets allowed. All with board approval. Laundry is in the building. The listing comes with its own basement. Which is a total bonus. Although, I understand there's currently a tenant living down there. He's got a lease. I'm not sure what the term is."

I raise an eyebrow at Ethan. He's a cop and I'm a prosecutor and I know we are both thinking the same things. Serial killer. Drug dealer. Insane child rapist.

Peter looks up from his sheet. "So that's about it. I'll leave you folks alone for a minute to discuss."

He withdraws to the other side of the room and checks his phone and pretends not to listen.

"So what do you think?" whispers Ethan, looking at me hopefully.

"You're kidding."

"Well, sure, it needs work. But I'm not afraid of that."

"Ethan, you can't be serious. We agreed that any house we buy has got to be fit for occupation with no major work required. We can't do renovations with a newborn."

"It's not that bad."

"Umm. Rotting floors. Mold. Lunatic tenant."

Ethan looks at me and exhales. "Yeah. You're probably right. It's not a good fit." He looks around, longingly. "Still, the potential…"

I rub his arm. "We'll get there."

*

11

Later, as we are waiting to be served at Bartholomew's, a cheap eats place that has quickly become a favorite while we've been saving for a place of our own, Ethan catches me checking the time on my watch.

"Want to get back to work, huh?" he says.

I feel a slight pull. I really need to review the files again but I don't have the heart to say so after his disappointment with the house.

"It can wait."

The waitress arrives and takes our order. A plate of chili with an extra side of guacamole for Ethan. Quesadilla, no cheese for me. I'm staying away from dairy and shellfish and most other foods these days because of the baby. There's a gigantic list of no-go items taped to my refrigerator. I was shocked when Dr. Liu first gave it to me.

"Even bean sprouts?" I had said. "What's wrong with those?"

"Salmonella," Sandy replied.

"And caffeine? You're kidding me?"

"A high caffeine intake during pregnancy has been shown to restrict fetal growth and increase the risk of low birth weight."

"But I can't function without coffee."

Sandy had smiled. "Just limit it to one a day."

So somehow my four-cup-a-day habit became one cup a day. My salads went without sprouts, and my quesadillas went without cheese. To make up for it, I plan on having a massive caffeine, sprout, and cheese party once the baby is born.

I stare at the bowl of tortilla chips and salsa in the center of the table.

"I should be okay with those, shouldn't I?" I say to Ethan. "No listeria hiding in there."

Ethan frowns at the salsa. "I don't know. Depends on what's in it."

I roll my eyes. "Come on, Ethan. It's just tomato."

I take a chip and dip it in the salsa, put it in my mouth, and crunch. It's good. Spicy.

"So, tomorrow," he says.

I exhale. "Yeah, tomorrow."

I reach for my glass of water, feel the coolness against my fingertips. He doesn't want me to go.

"I have to do it, Ethan, you know that," I say gently. "He insisted it be me."

The truth is, I want to go.

He nods and looks away. "You feel prepared?"

I take a sip of water. My lips are a little numb from the salsa. There must have been chili in it.

"One last review of the material tonight and I will be." I lower my eyes and my voice. "The confession is likely to take the full week. There's a lot to cover."

He nods but doesn't say anything.

"I'll only be a few hours away," I say.

"Yeah, locked in a small room in a state penitentiary with a vicious rapist and serial killer who's already tried to kill you twice." He pauses. "I wish you'd let me come."

"Ethan, I'll be there with two FBI agents, an armed guard, and Rex's lawyer. Nothing's going to happen to me."

He takes my hand across the table. "I'm proud of you, Amelia. I really am."

I feel myself blush at his unexpected praise.

13

"I've never seen anyone work so hard," he says, giving my hand a kiss.

*

Later when we are in bed locked in each other's arms, he whispers to me.

"Call me if you need me. Any little thing."

"I will."

"Promise me."

"I promise."

3

It's raining by the time FBI Special Agents Steve Novak and Laura March come to pick me up for the three-hour drive north to the Aken Correctional Facility. Raining and cold and dark because it's still only 5 a.m. on this pre-winter November morning. I give Novak and March a wave through the windshield, mouthing for them to stay put while Ethan places my overnight bag and box of files into the trunk of the black SUV. I stomp my feet against the cold as I wait under the umbrella and feel an unexpected rush of excitement. I tell myself not to be perverse. I'm about to interview a cold-blooded rapist and murderer—my rapist and would-be murderer at that. But the thought of finally getting some answers about what exactly happened to those twenty-five women is exhilarating. I can't help it. Almost fifteen months of planning and investigation and intense plea bargain negotiations are finally coming together.

Ethan shuts the trunk and turns to me, his breath a steam engine under the lamplight. It looks like he wants to say something.

"I'll be fine," I say.

He pulls me into an embrace. Holds me a little tighter than normal.

"Call me for anything," he says.

"You worry too much," I say. "Now go inside before you end up in ER with pneumonia."

He doesn't. Instead he stays on the street as we pull away, in the rain and the cold, standing there, watching us.

I lose sight of him when we round the corner and think about how difficult this is for him.

Novak yawns and looks at me in the rearview. "You okay with the backseat? We figured you could use the room."

Novak is always trying to joke about my pregnancy. I don't know why. I understand he's a perpetual bachelor type. He's never mentioned a wife and there's no wedding ring.

Novak rubs his five o'clock shadow and yawns again. A big wide-open noisy yawn that makes me want to tell him to keep his eyes on the road.

"Geez. Sorry," he says. "We flew in from Oregon last night. I didn't get much sleep at the crappy airport hotel. Then what do you know, March is banging on my door at the crack of dawn telling me it's time to get up."

March maintains a passive face. "It's a two-and-a-half-hour drive to Albany, sir."

Novak waves a hand. "Yeah, yeah. I get it, March. Punctuality is next to godliness."

If March is offended, she doesn't show it. A strict southern Baptist, the twenty-seven-year-old special agent is as conservative as they come. She is the perfect picture of Christian modesty, with shoulder-length brown hair neatly tied back, white shirt buttoned to the top, and gold necklace complete with dainty crucifix. I've never once seen March lose her temper or curse or be absolutely anything other than polite and gracious. No small feat given Novak's persistent attempts to provoke a reaction from her.

Compared to March, Novak comes across as eternally untidy and disorganized. Standing over six foot three, he is an imposing figure when he stands his full height with his shoulders back. He is attractive in a jaded sort of way, with deep-set hazel eyes and dark brown hair going gray at the temples. My best guess puts him at late forties, although he could be younger given the stresses of the job.

I first met them nearly a year ago when they were put in charge of the case after the Hawkins plea bargain had been reached. Although Hawkins had agreed to provide a full confession in return for the State of Oregon not pursuing the death penalty, it wasn't simply a case of taking his word for it. We needed to be sure he confessed to all the murders he was responsible for. We also needed to be sure that he was providing us with the correct location of the bodies. That meant gathering as much material as possible about the missing and murdered women—to flesh out the details of what we already knew about them, as well as uncover any other possible victims.

Thanks to March's diligence, we found five more. After seven months of trawling through twenty-plus years of archives and missing persons reports, March identified Melissa Barton (22); Julia Peters (19); Barbara Mitchell (20); Louise Fellows (20); and Jana Smith (21). A mix of hitchhikers, runners, and trekkers, the women fit the same physical and demographic profile of Rex Hawkins's other known victims and had vanished in similar circumstances. The commonalities were just too striking to ignore.

I look out the window as we breeze down the I-87 and think about our list of twenty-five women. I feel like I know every single one of them intimately. I know all their names and faces by heart. I have even met most of their families. The responsibility weighs heavily on me. But if I do nothing else in my life but this, bring their daughters and sisters home and provide answers to what happened, I will die a happy woman.

I feel pressure on my bladder and am reminded of my other responsibility. I look out the window for a passing gas station.

Then Novak says, "I need food."

I'm relieved. At least now I don't have to admit I need to stop for a pee, which would have no doubt unleashed Novak's teasing.

March glances at her watch.

Novak rolls his eyes. "Don't be such a nervous ninny, March. There's plenty of time and you of all people know how fast I can eat."

We pull up at a truck stop and enter the restaurant, where I draw stares from gray-whiskered truckers as I waddle and clap my way to the bathroom; a pregnant disabled lady is probably something they don't see every day. I get to the stall and do my thing and suddenly I'm hit with an unexpected wave of nausea. I pivot to fumble with the toilet seat and dry-retch into the bowl. The dreadful sound echoes off the porcelain back at me, which sets me off again. I heave painful, empty gasps. Over and over again until my sides ache and my throat's about to cave in.

Then, mercifully, it stops. I collapse back on my calves and try to catch my breath. I remind myself that pregnancy is not a permanent state of being and that one day very soon I will be holding a brand-new baby in my arms instead of this stone-cold toilet bowl.

There's a tap at the door.

"Are you all right, Ms. Kellaway? Can I get you anything?"

It's March. I imagine her standing there looking at her watch, biting her lip.

"I'll be right out, Laura."

I hear the door close as she exits. I wonder how I'm going to manage the interview if I get one of these surprise attacks. Did I remember to pack my nausea tablets? I must not under any circumstances forget to take them. They aren't always foolproof but usually help.

I sit there for a few minutes longer to gather myself. When I'm satisfied the episode has passed, I return to find Novak and March seated at the counter.

Novak looks at me, wiping his face with a napkin then dropping it into a plate smeared with egg yolk and remnants of sausage. He's finished already? Was I in the bathroom that long?

"Boy, you look like shit," he says.

"Thanks, Novak, just what I needed to hear."

"You sure you're gonna be okay to do the interview?"

I don't sit down. Instead I turn and head for the door. "I take it you're done stuffing your face, Novak. We don't want to be late."

4

We reach the prison just after 8 a.m. Located in the middle of nowhere behind a line of imposing firs, the compound is surrounded by electric chain-link fences with razor ribbon, on the other side of which lay miles of desolate land overrun with brush. A distinctive gloom hangs over the place, helped in no part by the miserable overcast sky that promises nothing but more of the same.

Built in the mid-1980s, Aken Correctional Facility was designed to house fifteen hundred medium security prisoners, and two hundred and five maximum security offenders. It is a sprawling complex of interconnected, windowless institutional blocks that could have easily been mistaken for a group of covert medical laboratories. I shudder as I look at it. There's no mistaking the wretchedness of the place. Hopelessness hangs in the air like smoke.

We reach a set of gates and Novak winds down the window to show the guard in the booth his identification. I glance up at the watchtower. Two guards, semi-automatics strapped over their shoulders, stare down at me unsmiling. Even from this distance, I can see one of the guards has a ghostly half-moon eye. I wonder if he's a returned veteran, exchanging one theater of war for another.

The guard waves us around to the left to the visitor car park and we pull into a space closest to the entrance. The rain starts, pelting noisily against the roof of the car. We shrug into our jackets and dash outside to retrieve the files and recording equipment from the trunk, doing our best to shield them from the rain battering our heads. I look down. The gravel parking lot is turning to mud.

Novak faces me and raises his voice over the noise. "Wait here! I don't want you slipping."

Before I can object, he and Marsh sprint inside the building with the boxes of hardcopy files and the hardcase with the portable interview recording system.

Novak returns to take my arm. "Don't get any ideas," he says, gingerly escorting me across the muddy parking lot and into the building. "I don't need another girlfriend."

Once inside, we go through the security check. First our personal bags are searched, then the individual components of the recording equipment—the mics and cords and camera and hard drive unit—every single piece is taken from their foam compartment and scrutinized closely. Next the hardcopy files are leafed through in detail. Even the boxes they came in are examined thoroughly.

Once that's done, a male guard takes Novak to a side room, and March and I are shown to another room where a female guard is waiting for us—a heavyset woman with a buzz cut and khaki trousers straining over big hips.

She breaks into a grin when she sees my belly. "You look like you're about to pop."

"Tell me about it," I say.

She asks me to starfish, and I stand there, arms out and legs astride, as she pats me down.

"As long as you don't got no bomb in there, you're good to go, hon."

I thank her and wait until March is given the all clear and we return to the reception area to find Novak waiting for us. We gather our things and follow a guard through a secure door and down a brightly lit corridor with badly scarred linoleum. The black baton attached to the guard's belt knocks against what looks like a canister of chemical spray and I wonder if he's ever had to use either.

We turn left and continue on. The further in we go, I more I experience the strange sensation of being underground even though we aren't. There's a mustiness to the place, and the noises of the prison, the clank of metal against metal, a cough or a shout or an abrupt cheerless laugh, seem flat and far away.

Finally we reach a cluster of rooms. A unisex staff toilet to the left. Three rooms to the right. Victor O'Leary, Rex Hawkins's lawyer, is waiting outside the middle room, thumbing through his phone. In his mid-sixties, the wolfish Texas native is blessed with a luscious full head of steel gray hair that he wears in a ponytail at the nape of his neck. Today Victor is dressed in his usual attire—a broad-brimmed, cream cowboy hat and button-up shirt complete with a leather bolo tie and silver turquoise slide. A death penalty expert, Victor is at the tail end of his career, and only takes cases that interest him. I suspect that representing one of America's worst serial killers was too big an opportunity to miss.

"Oh my, how you've grown, my dear," he says when he sees me.

"Good morning, Victor."

"Brought the cavalry, I see," he says, eyes passing over Novak and March.

"You're early," snaps Novak. "You'll need to wait outside until we set up the equipment."

Victor smiles. "Whatever you say, Special Agent Novak. I'll just play Candy Crusher on my phone."

I don't want the proceedings to become antagonistic this early on so I give Victor a gracious nod. "Thank you, Victor. We shouldn't be long."

The guard unlocks the door to the interview room and a wall of heat hits us. It's so hot the cinderblock walls are sweating.

"Could you turn down the thermostat, please?" I say to the guard.

I glance around. The room is small and plain and windowless. Beige-painted walls. Air conditioner duct snaking overhead. Overly bright fluorescent strip lighting. In the center of the room is a large table with four plastic chairs. I turn to March.

"Laura, can you find another two chairs? We're going to need them for Victor and the guard."

March disappears out the door and Novak lays the hardcase on the table and he and I set up the recording equipment.

Twenty minutes later, we are all set to go. There is water and plastic cups. The equipment has been tested and works. My notes are in front of me. I have taken my nausea tablets. Everyone is clear on their roles. As I survey the room like some sort of nervous wedding planner, I realize I'm shaking.

The guard pokes his head around the door at exactly 9 a.m. "Want me to go get him, ma'am?"

I nod.

We sit there and wait.

5

I spent five sessions with an FBI criminal profiler to prepare for the plea interview. John Liber, my boss, had insisted.

"You've already been to hell and back with this son-of-a-bitch, kiddo, and I want you to be prepared for any mind games he might play."

I didn't object. I needed all the help I could get. So this September I began my fortnightly four-hour Amtrak train trips to see Jane Duffy at the FBI Academy in the Marine Corps base in Quantico, Virginia. Originally a psychoanalyst specializing in couples' therapy, Jane had switched to criminal profiling in the early 1980s. Now world renown for her encyclopedic knowledge in the field, she has run the FBI's profiling department for the last twenty years.

When I arrived on the first visit, Jane was there to greet me at reception.

"Hello, dear," she said, taking my hand in hers. "You must be the famous Amelia Kellaway. It's such a pleasure to meet you."

I was surprised by her warmth and genuine smile. A bird-like woman with very tiny wrists, Jane was dressed in a black turtleneck and black tailored trousers. There was a timeless elegance about her, and if I hadn't known she was seventy-three, I would have put her at late fifties. It was difficult to picture this soft-spoken woman interviewing some of America's worst serial killers. More difficult still to think of someone holding onto their own humanity when their daily life involved traversing the darkest corners of the human mind.

She opened a door to the left. "Shall we?"

I followed her outside and we took a winding pathway toward her office, Jane patiently keeping in step with me and my cane as we went. Looking around as we walked, I took in the sprawling campus. It was a beautiful place and bordered by magnificent oaks, poplars, and maples. The morning air was fresh and taut. In the distance, shots rang out from a firing range.

We reached her office and the first thing I noticed when we entered was Anthony Hopkins's demented face glaring down at us from a large framed poster of *Silence of the Lambs*.

"A gift from my students," said Jane, eyes twinkling.

I took in the rest of her office. Wall-to-wall bookcases were populated by her own works and those of other notable experts. Carl Jung. Sigmund Freud. Viktor Frankl. John Douglas. Robert Ressler. Roy Hazelwood. To the left there was a flat-screen TV. Above that, shelving full of DVDs. To the right, a large floor-to-ceiling window overlooked a grassed courtyard area and provided a good dose of daylight onto what would otherwise be a dark corner office.

"Please sit," she said, gesturing to the comfy-looking armchair.

She poured us both a coffee from the sideboard and lowered herself into a well-worn executive chair.

"They gave me a file to read," she said. "About you."

I felt a sting of betrayal. "Okay."

"They were concerned about your psychological welfare. Whether you could cope with what's being asked of you."

I tried to keep a neutral face but inside I was humiliated. "John means well. But he can be overprotective," I said.

She nodded. "I agree." She laced her delicate fingers together. "The very fact that you're here with your shoulders back tells me you more than survived. You came through the storm and went on to thrive. I'm not here to give you therapy, Amelia, I'm here to teach you how to get every last drop of information you can from Rex Hawkins."

"That's what I want, too."

She smiled. "Good. Then let's get started." She slid a thick file across the desk. "The three psychiatric reports Hawkins has undergone in the last twelve months."

I'm surprised. "He agreed to that?"

She shrugged. "By all accounts, he's been cooperative and open and highly motivated."

I frowned. "Isn't he just trying to manipulate things?"

"Oh, undoubtedly, my dear. But that doesn't mean there aren't valuable insights to be gained from the reports." She tapped the file. "He's fairly typical of his cohort, actually. Rich interior fantasy life—rage and sex mixed together. Early life of neglect, abandonment, and abuse. Delusions of grandeur. 'I'm all powerful. I know things no one else does. I'm smarter than all of you put together.' His mission is to seek out and destroy the feminine archetype."

"Why do you think he hates women so much?"

Jane exhaled. "We could go down a rabbit hole explaining that one. Freud, in particular, has some enlightening theories, but simply put, at his core, Rex Hawkins feels deeply inadequate. Women make him feel intensely self-conscious and he hates them for it. He wants to punish and exact revenge against the fairer sex." Jane tapped the pen on her top lip and looked thoughtful. "What is interesting, though, is his almost paternal impulse coupled with the need to hurt. A push and pull, if you will. I'm talking about his pattern of abduction and the acting out of the fantasy that he and his victim will live happily together in isolation." She looked at me. "You can relate to that?"

I nodded. "Definitely. At times during the abduction, he could be almost tender, apologetic even, then he'd turn on a dime with the most horrible violence." I shuddered at the memory.

Jane stared out the window. "There is still so much we don't understand. We used to think that most, if not all, serial killers were white, not black. We used to think most were antisocial loners. But a lot of the early research has turned out, how shall I put it? Misguided? For instance, a large proportion of serials are in functional relationships with women, and even have children in many cases. And opposed to being antisocial, many are productive community members. In fact, I understand that Hawkins himself was quite philanthropic and highly regarded by his community. Also, the entire black/white thing turned out to be a fallacy. Samuel Little, an African American, recently admitted to ninety murders and is one of the most prolific serial killers in US criminal history."

"Do you think it's possible that Rex is genuinely remorseful?"

Jane gestured to her bookshelf. "The literature on psychopathy is changing. The old view was that psychopaths don't possess a conscience. But the more I'm in this job, the less I believe in the idea that psychopaths are solely without feeling and empathy. So too, the idea that psychopaths can never change. There's some exciting research on the elasticity of the brain that shows great promise in terms of rewiring disordered neuro-pathways. So yes, I think it could be possible—Rex could feel remorse. But that doesn't make him any less dangerous. I suggest his impulses far outweigh any limited effect episodes of remorse may have. And it is possible, in fact likely even, that he has not one iota of remorse at all. It could be that the plea bargain and confession is his way to show how clever he was to get away with so much for so long. To go down in the history books as one of the worst serial killers and all that…" She looked at me squarely, her blue eyes contemplating. "No, I think there's more to it than that. I think it's about you. His relationship with you. His obsession with you is fascinating. It's not a situation that I have come across before, and I believe it's something you can use to your advantage. I suspect he will try and impress you with what he sees as his sheer brilliance."

"So you think it's possible to predict his behavior?"

She took a breath. "I think, my dear, it would be a mistake to think we can ever understand him. Your best approach is quite the opposite. Take the stance you know nothing and let him reveal himself to you. Discovery, not validation, see what I mean? That way he gives you the maximum amount of information and detail. That way he thinks he's the one in control. You get the picture?"

I nodded. "I do."

Jane raises herself from her seat. "Now," she said. "Let me show you the interview room."

I followed her down the corridor and she opened a door on the left. The room was small and white-walled, pretty much the usual interrogation space you might find in a typical police station.

Jane pointed to the table and seating, which had been set up in an L-shape.

"Any good architect will tell you the arrangement of space is of prime importance as to how human beings interact with each other," she said, placing her hands on the back of one of the chairs. "An interview situation is no different. We want to maximize comfort and minimize friction. No face-to-face across a table—that's too confrontational—instead, seat him at the top of the L and you at a right angle next to him, almost side-on. It's far more collaborative."

"What about eye contact? Should I avoid that?"

"On the contrary, eye contact is good. It shows him you are paying attention and he definitely wants attention. The one exception is if you think he's being deceptive. Look away then. It will convey your doubt about what he's saying and he's likely to want to pull you back in. He'll be watching you closely for what he can get away with. If he knows you're onto him, he'll likely revert to the truth or something close to it. And don't worry about showing emotion—disgust, sadness, whatever—it doesn't matter. Part of this whole thing is he wants to see your human reaction to what he's done. The more authentic you are, the more he'll reveal."

"How will I know if he's being deceptive or not?"

Jane took a seat at the top of the table. "That's where all your background work on the case comes in. Know the file inside and out and you'll naturally pick up things that don't ring true. Listen to your gut. There could be other signs, too. Ventilation, for instance, which is this—" She tugged at the collar of her shirt. "It indicates stress. I've also sometimes seen leg cleansing, where they rub their palms along the tops of their legs. But more often than not, with serials there is no sign. They are masters of self-control. If at some point you do believe he's being deceptive, avoid direct questions or he's likely to close up. Instead say, 'I don't understand something. Help me to understand. What have I got wrong?' Put the emphasis on you. But be careful. He's smart. And he knows you're smart, too. If he suspects you're trying to manipulate him, he won't be happy. He has to believe he's the one with the power, the one in control."

I must have looked apprehensive because Jane took my hand.

"You can do this," she said.

"I hope so."

"Oh, you can, my dear. I'm certain of it. Just remember, above all else, show him respect."

6

As we wait for Rex to arrive, the rain continues to fall. Droplets blur and skid down the tiny window high up near the ceiling. It looks cold outside, not like in here. In here, it's still nuclear, despite the guard tinkering with the thermostat. I lick my lips and take a sip of water. Perhaps it's just me. Perhaps I shouldn't have gone for the woolen turtleneck and heavy trouser combo. I should have layered. I should have worn the simple blue maternity dress with the navy cardigan instead.

I look at my watch and wonder what's taking so long. For one terrible moment, I think he's changed his mind. That the plea deal is off. That he's in his cell right now refusing to come out.

Settle, I tell myself. I'm being ridiculous. If he doesn't confess, he's looking at the death penalty. He wants this as much as we do. He'll be here. I just need to be patient and calm the heck down.

Behind me the door opens and there's a sudden whoosh of dank, stale air and the jangle of chains. The hairs on the back of my neck stand on end. I can't turn around. I know he's there. I feel the weight of him in the room, sucking the air from the place like a sponge. Instead I focus on my hands and take a deep breath through my nose and out through my mouth and hope that no one notices how nervous I am. Then, suddenly, he's right there in front of me, looking.

I lift my gaze. "Hello, Rex."

His eyes drop to my belly and he smiles broadly. "Oh, Amelia, you're going to be a mama! I'm so happy for you, truly I am."

Right on cue, my blood pressure monitor beeps and I fumble to set it to silent.

"Thank you, Rex," I say, fighting the urge to lay a protective hand across my pregnant belly. "Why don't you take a seat."

He slides into the plastic chair to my right, just as I had rehearsed with Jane. It's strange, seeing him. He's like a long-lost relative who's returned from a faraway journey, familiar yet different somehow. I don't know what I expected, but not this. Not this calm and relaxed everyday man. Not this placid, almost entirely gray-haired, serene older citizen. I search for the latent rage behind his eyes, but it isn't there. He looks…well, he looks kind.

And put together, in his prison-issued regulation khaki uniform, with his blindingly white T-shirt beneath the starched box shirt with precise, sharp creases along the sleeves. And dare I say it, he looks obedient, sitting there in the hard-backed chair, forearms resting on the table in front of him, wrists cuffed and connected to a belly-chain wrapped around his waist, hands clutching a small maroon-colored King James bible. I watch him caress the Good Book with his thumb, back and forth, slowly, lovingly, and wonder if it's just for show.

This apparent transformation of cold-blood killer to born-again Christian does nothing to quell my biological predator-fear system, and my tendons and muscles and fast-twitch fibers are tightening to near breaking point. My heart batters against my ribcage. I can't help it. My subconscious sees him as a threat. He might as well be a poisonous snake as far as my limbic system's concerned.

I'm angry at myself. I thought I was past all this. I know I am safe here, that he can't hurt me, that I can take care of myself should anything happen. Still, it rattles me, seeing him face-to-face like this. I try not to let it show. Relax your mouth, God damn it, breathe through your nose, swallow the tension in your throat. Don't let him see.

At the end of the table Novak shifts, growing impatient. I've warned him not to talk. We have to stick to the strategy and let Rex take the lead.

Rex turns his head. "And who do we have here?"

He stares at March for a beat. She has that startled deer-in-the-headlights look on her face. A moustache of condensation glistens on her top lip and I fight the urge to wipe it away. I wonder what he sees. A young nubile victim? A slender neck to strangle? Or am I being too judgmental now that he's a God-fearing man?

I clear my throat. "Special Agents Novak and March have been leading the investigation and may have some questions for you."

My voice sounds weaker than I would have liked. I reach for my water then decide against it, better to not reveal my shaking hands.

Victor O'Leary tuts. "I think you'll find it clearly defined in the plea agreement that Mr. Hawkins will only speak to you, Ms. Kellaway." O'Leary flicks through his copy of the plea agreement, runs a finger down to tab A, then pauses to read. "Yes, it's right here. Paragraph 23.1."

I push back. "Special Agents Novak and March need to be present. They're in charge of the recovery of the bodies back in Oregon. There could be points of clarification they require. Surely that's permissible under the circumstances?"

O'Leary shrugs. "It's not what was agreed to."

Novak makes a guttural noise in his throat. I shoot him a stern look.

"I can assure you, Mr. O'Leary, Special Agents Novak and March are not here to interfere."

But O'Leary won't be moved. "No, no, this won't do at all. You can't just rewrite the agreement to suit yourself, Ms. Kellaway. This has taken months to negotiate, as you well know. Everything has been discussed, agreed to, and signed off. Mr. Hawkins is here to honor his part and expects you to do the same."

Rex holds up his hand. "They can stay, Vic. It's of no consequence to me."

O'Leary frowns his disapproval. "We really should adhere to the agreement, Rex. It's there for your protection, too."

Rex leans back in his chair. "I'm not here to create barriers. I'm here to speak the truth, to make amends as far as I can. Besides, I've always known Amelia to be a straight shooter. There's no trickery on your part, is there, Amelia?"

I look at him. "Absolutely not."

"That's settled then," says Rex, closing the matter. "Shall we begin?"

"I would appreciate that," I say.

O'Leary shuts the plea agreement in a huff. "Well, consider yourself advised, Rex."

"Yes, Vic. I surely will."

Everyone looks at me expectantly. The floor is all mine. It's unnerving having all eyes on me but I do my best to push that aside.

"Before we begin recording the interview, there are some things I need to cover with you." I look down at my notes. "In terms of the interview structure, I'll first read a formal introduction into the record, then ask you to state your name, age, and address. From there, it's over to you, although it would be beneficial to us if you could walk us through events chronologically in as much detail as possible." I glance at my watch. "We'll take a break at eleven a.m., then again at two p.m. We have the room booked for the rest of the week so we can take our time. Once the interview is complete, each incident will be written up in a summary of facts document. You'll get the opportunity to review the document to ensure its accuracy. If you're happy with it, sign it. After that the summary of facts will be submitted to the court for the day of your pleading." I look up to see Rex listening intently. "Do you understand?"

"I do, Amelia, thank you," he says.

"Do you have any questions before we begin the video recording?"

He shakes his head. "I do not."

I give March a nod and like a good lieutenant she nods back and clicks the record button. The hard drive whirs into life. I pick up my pre-prepared statement and after stating the date and time, I proceed with the introduction.

"This is a recording of an interview with Rex David Hawkins. The parties present are Special Agents Steve Novak and Laura March; counsel for the defendant, Victor O'Leary; the defendant, Rex David Hawkins; and myself,

Assistant District Attorney Amelia Kellaway. Mr. Hawkins, can you please state your full name, date of birth, and address for the record?"

"Rex David Hawkins, November third, 1958. I currently reside at the Aken Correctional facility in Albany, New York."

"Mr. Hawkins, do you confirm that the statement you are about to give is pursuant to the agreement reached with the State of Oregon in which you have agreed to plead guilty to an as yet unspecified number of counts of aggravated murder in the first degree?"

"That is correct."

"Do you confirm that part of this agreement is to provide us with the details of the elements of each count, including the location of the victims' bodies where necessary?"

"That is correct."

"Mr. Hawkins, do you understand that you have the right to representation by a lawyer and that you are, in actual fact, legally represented here today?"

He nods. "Yes, I understand my rights, and Mr. O'Leary, my legal counsel, is present here with me today."

"Finally, Mr. Hawkins, can you confirm that the statement you are about to give is the truth, the whole truth, and nothing but the truth?"

He places his hand on the little bible, cloaking the entire thing. "I do."

"You may begin."

7

The room falls quiet as we wait for Rex to commence with his confession. He lowers his eyes and studies the floor. I fight the urge to fill the silence. I know this is part of it—his game, his need for control. He's priming us, the audience, building anticipation like any good performer would.

He raises his eyes and looks at me. "Firstly, Amelia, I want to say how sorry I am, sorry for what I did to you. I'm sorry I hurt you. I'm sorry that you've had to live with the consequences of what happened and how it has affected your life, and so on and so forth. There's a darkness in me that I don't understand. It's like I have a sewer in the seat of my soul. Sometimes it takes over and makes me do the most terrible things." He exhales. "But with the help of the Lord I'm beginning to understand the darkness is not all there is to me. That I'm more than that. That I can be and do better. In short, I've realized that I'm a child of God, just like you." He hesitates. "I've never told anyone this before, but that night in your apartment when you shot me, a miracle happened. I died for near on five minutes before they brought me back to life. Amelia, I saw the most beautiful light. It was the most glorious thing I ever did see. And the Lord spoke to me, Amelia, he told me it was not my time, that I needed to go back and make amends to those I hurt." Tears glisten in his eyes. "I know I've destroyed many lives but I want to put it right as much as I can. I'm not asking for your forgiveness, I wouldn't burden you with that, my hope instead is that by telling you how sorry I am for what I did, to you and to all the other women, that it helps with your healing."

Bullshit, I want to say. To hell with your false platitudes and self-serving lies. You're a cold-blooded murderer and rapist and you enjoyed every minute of it.

"I'm here for the victims and their families, Rex. Period. Your religious transformation or otherwise is of no concern to me—with all due respect, of course."

He stares at his hands. "I understand why you feel that way, Amelia, I really do. You have no reason to believe me. Why would you after everything I've done? But I want you to know that I am being sincere."

"We're here to listen, not judge." I'm pleased with myself. That one was right out of the profiler's toolbox.

"Thank you, Amelia," says Rex. "You'll never know how much I appreciate that." He shifts his arms and the chains grate noisily against the corner of the table. "It isn't easy to talk about. I feel so much shame."

I nod. "Take your time."

He closes his eyes for a second and draws a breath.

Eventually, he lifts his gaze. "There were twenty-seven. Plus you."

I glance at March. One more than we originally thought. "Go on," I say.

He frowns to himself. "I've been trying to remember their names, the dates, details. It's hard when so much time has passed. But I do remember the first one. She was named Belinda."

I open my folder and take out a photo. His eyes drop to the face of the smiling nineteen-year-old woman.

"Yes. That's her," he says.

Belinda Smith. Date of birth—February 16, 1963. One sister and two brothers. Missing, presumed dead.

"Can you remember the exact date of the incident?"

"Thursday, November third, 1982. It was my twenty-fourth birthday. I picked her up along the I-5 outside of Eugene. People...women...hitchhiked a lot back then. She was a nice person. Pretty, too. She had this wristwatch. A Casio, I think. I remember that because I'd never seen a digital watch before. She smelled like baby talc. It was so hot out and she was real happy to get into a car with air conditioning. Ten minutes after I picked her up, I pulled into a rest area."

He pauses.

"Yes?" I say.

He gives me a blank look. "I don't remember what came next."

Jane Duffy had warned me about this—the potential for Rex to feign a memory lapse. She advised me not to challenge him in case he clammed up so I wait for him to continue.

Rex glances at me. "I know what you're thinking, that I'm trying to avoid responsibility and so on and so forth, but I'm not. I know I must have killed her."

"What's the next thing you remember?" I ask.

"Looking down and seeing Ms. Smith's dead body."

"When you say looking down, what do you mean?"

"I was on top of her, in the passenger seat. There were bruises on her neck. Her face was blue. Her tongue..." he makes a gesture with his hands and pulls a disgust face, "was swelling up like crazy."

"Did you sexually assault her?"

"I don't remember."

"Were her clothes on or off when you came to?"

He pauses. "Off below the waist."

"So it's reasonable to assume you sexually assaulted her?"

O'Leary sighs. "Ms. Kellaway, Mr. Hawkins has already said he doesn't remember."

Rex interjects. "No, Vic. It's all right. I accept that I must have."

"What did you do with the body?" I say.

"I buried it in the woods."

"Do you remember where?"

He nods. "I can show you."

Novak rises from his seat to retrieve a portfolio of satellite images and a large map of the Oregon area. He unfurls the map and places it in front of Rex. Rex traces his finger along the blue line that represents the 1-5 until he reaches Eugene, then he moves right, following the road inland toward Lowell.

He taps the map. "There," he says. "You'll find her about a hundred yards in, the third rest area along the road. I recall some sort of statue, a stone memorial, Indian maybe. I can't be sure."

Novak holds out a pen. "Mark it."

Rex does as instructed. Novak unfurls the satellite image and has Rex mark that, too. Once he's done, Rex sits back in his chair and looks at me.

"It was a long time ago now, Amelia. With animals and what-not, well…she may not all be there."

I think I detect genuine sadness but can't be sure.

"Anything's better than nothing," I say. "The families need closure and this will help."

"Well, that's my intention, Amelia, to help. The best way I can."

Rex picks up the photo of Belinda Smith and looks at it solemnly.

"She was a nice person," he says, more to himself than to anyone else. "She didn't deserve what happened." He places the photo face down on the table. "If I could take it back, I would."

I long to ask him about remorse, what he did in the days and weeks after, whether he was racked by guilt. Then, as if reading my thoughts, he says—

"I completely shut out what happened and never considered it again." He reaches for the water in front of him and takes a sip. "Does that trouble you, Amelia?" he says, looking at me over the rim of the plastic cup.

"It doesn't matter what I think."

He seems mildly offended. "It matters to me."

He lowers his cup and falls silent and I wonder if I've blown it. If Belinda Smith is all we're ever going to get.

"Maybe your mind was protecting you from what happened," I say, reaching for a connection. "It's possible that a coping mechanism could have been at play."

Rex looks at me, contemplating. "That's kind of you to say, Amelia, and such a nice way of seeing the world." His eyes shift toward Novak, whose distaste is clearly displayed on his face. "I suspect Special Agent Novak doesn't share your point of view. I suspect he's thinking that the only thing at play here was a psychopath who couldn't care less about the fact he'd just killed some innocent human being. Isn't that right, Special Agent Novak? A psychopath with no conscience? No feelings? No remorse? Well, I'm here to tell you that isn't true. I am sorry. More than any of you

41

will ever know." Rex bends his head and stares at his bible. "But that's between me and the Lord now."

Novak bristles. "Stop with the sermonizing, Hawkins, and get on with it."

Rex looks at Novak evenly. "You wanted me to talk, so I'm talking."

I shift in my seat. The last thing I want is for this to devolve into some type of sparring match.

"Let's not lose focus, everyone. There's a lot we need to get through," I say.

O'Leary chimes in. "Perhaps we should take a break."

Novak barks out a laugh. "A break? That's totally out of the question. We've only covered one murder. At this rate we'll be sitting here for six months." He shakes his head, adamant. "No break. We keep going."

Rex waves a hand. "It's all right, Vic. I'm fine."

"You hear that, O'Leary?" says Novak. "Your client is fine."

"Okay, Novak," I warn.

To my relief, Novak leans back in his chair and finally shuts his mouth.

I turn to Rex. "Let's continue, shall we? Who was next?"

Rex looks at me directly. "Shelly White. Near on a year later."

Shelly White, thirty-two years old. The first woman I identified as a possible victim of Rex's. Ten days after she was reported missing by her boyfriend, Shelly's body was found in a shallow grave. The autopsy revealed she'd been the victim of a sustained sexual assault, the cause of death strangulation.

"I had taken a few days off for a fishing trip and was camping along the Montana-Oregon border when this woman appeared out of nowhere. She was a little bitty thing. Upset as hell." Rex looks at March. "You remind me of her actually, sweetheart. You've got the same soft, pretty eyes." March goes red. I feel her discomfort and try to steer the conversation back to Shelly White.

"Go on."

"She said her name was Shelly. She was lost, had a fight with her boyfriend, or some such thing, and had been wandering out in the woods for hours. It was getting dark and she was scared. She'd been crying. I felt sorry for her."

I imagine Shelly's misguided relief at stumbling upon Rex and his campsite. No doubt, she would have thought he was her way out of there.

"What happened next?"

Rex shrugs. "We talked. Had coffee. It was nice." He looks at me pointedly. "I wasn't out to hurt anybody. She asked if we could leave. I told her it was too dark to drive. I said I didn't know the area too well and didn't want to risk getting lost."

"You lied."

"I was lonely. I wanted company. I promise you, at the time, that was all I was after."

"But something changed?"

He goes quiet.

"Did you black out again?"

He shakes his head. "I did not."

"Okay."

He searches my face. "Do the details really matter, Amelia? I admit I did it, isn't that enough?"

"You know it isn't, Rex," I say.

"The plea deal requires you provide a full account of your offenses," says Novak, sharply. "So that's exactly what you're gonna do."

I shoot Novak a frown to quiet him. Rex lifts his eyes to the ceiling and lets out a long, heavy breath.

Finally, he says, "All right. I'll tell you. We went to sleep and the next thing I know I'm being shaken awake. It's Ms. White, hissing in my ear that she's heard something in the woods. She thinks it's a bear. The woman is frightened out of her wits and seeing her like that, I don't know, something came over me...the darkness...I can't begin to explain it."

"Go on."

"I took her right then and there."

"Took her?"

"Had sex with her," says Rex.

"You raped her."

He pauses. "It was without her consent, yes."

"What happened next?" I say.

"She tried to get away. Fought like hell, as a matter of fact. Scratched me nice and deep on the cheek." He looks at me. "She was a fighter, Amelia."

I feel a chill go up my spine. That's what he had called me.

"Then you killed her?"

He nods and flexes his hands. "The same way as before."

"By strangulation?"

He nods again.

I think of Shelly White's last moments. I think of Rex's murderous hands around her neck. Then I think of them around mine, choking the life from me, the vile look of uncontrolled rage in his eyes as he was doing it.

"I'm not proud of what happened by any stretch. But there it is," he says. He looks at me and frowns. "Why Amelia, you've gone as white as a ghost."

I open my mouth to say something but nothing comes out.

"Are you all right, Ms. Kellaway?" says March, brow wrinkling.

Somehow I manage to find my voice. "I'm fine."

"Maybe we should take five after all," says Rex.

I shake my head, annoyed. "Please, everyone—I'm absolutely fine." I shuffle my notes on the table in front of me. "Please continue, Rex."

He stares at me. "If you're sure, Amelia."

"I am."

He nods slowly. "All right then, I know you're a woman who knows her own mind, so I won't disagree." He pauses. "Now, where was I?"

"Number three."

"Ah yes, number three. I do believe number three was a woman named Delia Leigh."

8

It's after nine p.m. by the time we take a seat at the diner across from our motel. The place is nearly empty apart from an off-duty prison guard nursing a steaming mug of coffee and a slice of lemon meringue pie at the counter. A pretty waitress with a shiny auburn ponytail and name tag that says Becky K bounces over to take our order. I expect to see Novak's usual flirtatious display, something he typically does whenever he encounters an attractive woman, but tonight he's subdued and doesn't even raise his eyes from the menu as he orders a Diet Coke and chicken melt on rye. I order a club sandwich, and March opts for a chicken salad with croutons. Once Becky is through taking our orders, the three of us retreat into silence, staring out the window into the wet, black night.

Novak's the first to speak, washing his face with his hands. "Jesus, this guy's a fucking monster."

So far Rex has confessed to five rapes and murders, and given us the location of each of their graves. And he's just getting started.

I glance at March. I'm worried about her. She looks wrung out. Her near translucent skin seems even paler, if that's at all possible, and this morning's youthful zeal has been replaced with a dark haunted look. I know this is her first murder.

"How are you holding up?" I ask.

"I'm fine, Ms. Kellaway. I mean, it's certainly tough to hear, but we've got to focus on the good we're doing."

46

"That may be so but this is just day one and it's only going to get harder from this point on. No one's going to think less of you if you need some time out."

March nods. "Thank you, Ms. Kellaway, but I've got this."

Novak stabs the plastic gingham tablecloth with a fork. "March is tougher than you think, Amelia. She may look like a delicate waterstone lily, but don't be fooled. She once saved my life by tackling an armed offender about to blow my head off. By the way, March, I don't think I ever thanked you for that."

"You're welcome, sir."

We lapse into silence again. My thoughts drift to Angela King, the last victim Rex mentioned today. He could barely remember anything about her. Worse still, Angela hadn't even been reported missing in the first place. Unlike the others, she was a prostitute with no fixed abode, and with no family and friends to speak of, there was no one to notice her absence. It was only after her body was found in scrubland along an Oregon back road did anyone even realize she'd been missing at all. It was so sad. I couldn't imagine how a person could become so invisible and forgotten.

There's a clatter and I look up to see Becky K arrive with our meals.

"About time," says Novak.

I'm about to scold him for being rude when I see him smiling at Becky K, eyes twinkling. Coloring at the attention, the poor girl places our plates in front of us, then stands back.

"Can I get you folks anything else?"

"Your phone number," says Novak, grinning.

Becky K goes redder.

"Ignore him," I say.

Becky K glances at Novak with a shy smile and then retreats to safety behind the counter.

I shake my head. "You're impossible…bordering on creepy."

He shrugs. "I try."

I look down at my club sandwich. "I forgot—I'm not supposed to eat ham."

"I'll have it," says Novak, shoveling his chicken melt into his mouth.

I pick out the ham and dump it on Novak's plate, leaving only a few shreds of limp lettuce, a teaspoon's worth of egg, and a smattering of mayo. But it's better than nothing, not that I have much of an appetite after today.

"Do you think he means it?" says March, picking at her salad. "The conversion?"

Novak rolls his eyes. "March, you can't be serious."

She touches the gold crucifix around her neck. "He seemed sincere."

"Don't be naïve," says Novak. "It's a total act."

"But what would he get out of pretending?"

"I don't know, March, maybe he just likes messing with us. Maybe it's a control thing. Maybe he wants us to feel sorry for him. But it's all bullshit, isn't that right, Amelia?"

They look at me. I hesitate. I'd rather not be referee in some ideological debate, and I don't want to offend March, but I think Novak is right.

"We will probably never understand how Rex Hawkins's mind works," I say, channeling Jane Duffy. "But right now, he's motivated to tell us everything so we should all be thankful for that."

"Amen to that," says Novak, throwing a crust onto his plate. "I'm done here." He glances at our mostly untouched meals. "If you guys aren't eating, I say we get the hell out of here."

*

We part ways and agree to meet at reception first thing in the morning. I'm thankful that my room is on the lower floor because hauling myself up a flight of stairs with my half-foot and cane is not something I have the energy for tonight. It's down to March, I suspect, as she's the one who booked the accommodations. I make a mental note to thank her for her kindness in the morning.

My room is clean and tidy, but basic. The gold-fringed bedspread has seen better days and I fold it up and put in on the chair because I don't want to think about how many bodies must have slept under it over the years.

I'm just about to take a shower when Ethan calls. I smile when I hear his voice.

"How's my favorite baby-momma doing?" he says.

"Tired."

"Tough day?"

"Yeah."

"Can I ask how it went?" he ventures.

I lower myself on the end of the bed. "Harrowing, actually."

"I bet."

"He found God."

"Oh, did he now?"

"Apparently. Can we talk about something else? What about you? How was your day?"

"I found another apartment for us to look at."

"Oh, that's terrific, Ethan."

"Views of the Hudson."

"Really?"

"No."

"Funny guy."

"I do my best. How's the young'un doing?"

I glance at my wrist. The monitor went off five times today, the most ever, but I don't tell Ethan this.

"Good. No dramas. Baby's kicking like crazy. Don't worry, I have no intention of giving birth inside a prison."

"Don't joke," he says. "Your mom called."

"Yeah? What did she want?"

"About her check-up, remember? You promised you would go with her. Next week."

"I completely forgot."

"Surprise."

"Hey, I've been a little busy."

"Don't I know it."

"Ethan."

"What?"

"Don't start."

I hear him breathing. "Hey, no starting going on here. Just saying, that's all."

I drop it. "I'm hoping to done with this thing by Friday."

"That long?"

"There's a lot to cover."

We go silent.

"I should let you go then," he says. "Get some sleep."

"Yeah. Thanks." I pause. "I love you."

"Right back at you."

*

I wake up at 3 a.m. This time the dream is not about Lorna and her teal blue rug. It's about me and Rex. In the woods. Sitting around a campfire. I blink into the darkness. His voice is rough in my ear.

"After the first one, Amelia, you never go back."

9

There's a sprinkle of rain during our short fifteen-minute ride to Aken for day two of the interview. I wonder if the inmates have any idea how beautiful it looks out here, with the majestic firs and birds bouncing on the powerlines with their puffed-out chests. Novak's hair is still wet from his morning shower. He looks drawn. March does, too. I don't blame them. I also feel wrung out and exhausted.

We go through the same admission process as yesterday, although it's a different female guard this time. Less jovial than the one the day before. No endearing comments about my belly. A little rougher in the pat down. Then we are shown through the same labyrinth of corridors by a thickset guard named Duane.

"You gettin' what you need, ma'am?' he says, hovering too close for my liking. "You know, from Hawkins?"

I give him a tight smile. "Everything's progressing fine, thank you."

"Well, you just let me know if that changes. I can always apply a little pressure for you." He flashes me a smile. "Unofficially, of course."

Novak catches my eye and gives me a playful smirk.

"That won't be necessary, Duane, but thank you," I say.

He nods. "Your call, ma'am. Hawkins thinks he's a big shot round here. But he's nothing to me. They do that sometimes, the inmates, forget who's in charge. Me and my boys have to give them a reminder every now and again. You know, to assert our authority."

"They're like monkeys, aren't they, these degenerates," says Novak, feigning disgust.

Duane nods. "You bet they are. No better than monkeys and dogs."

We reach the interview room and Duane unlocks the door.

"There you go, ma'am. Make yourself comfortable and I'll go get Hawkins for you." He gives me parting smile, flashing some seriously bad teeth, and heads off down the corridor.

"I think someone has a crush," says Novak, grinning.

"Don't go there."

He shrugs. "Just saying, that's all. If things don't work out between you and Ethan…"

I ignore him and put my bag on the table. O'Leary hasn't arrived yet so March and Novak take the opportunity to check the recording equipment while I review my notes. At about five to nine, O'Leary appears at the door, shaking raindrops from his coat. He looks tired.

"You're late," says Novak, without looking up.

"Traffic," says O'Leary.

"Bullshit. Your motel is closer to Aken than ours."

"Okay, you two," I say, looking at them both. "Everyone's a little on edge. This isn't easy on any of us, including you, Victor. But low-level squabbling is only going to make things worse."

There's the jangle of chains and the door opens. I feel myself stiffen, and that predator-fear system of mine begins firing like crazy again. Swallowing down the fear, I force myself to turn around.

"Good morning, Amelia."

"Good morning, Rex," I say, giving him a nod in return.

He looks the most well-rested out of everyone. Shirt as clean and crisp as yesterday. Freshly shaven. Eyes clear. He's brought his bible again and I wonder if he plans on quoting passages at some point. Jane said that might happen.

Duane escorts Rex to his seat and then takes up his position near the corner by the door.

I look at Rex. "Shall we begin? We've got a lot to get through."

He nods. "Of course, Amelia."

March turns on the recording equipment, and I read a statement into the record outlining that this is day two of proceedings.

I nod at Rex. "Please continue on from yesterday."

He blinks at the ceiling. "Where was I? I forget."

"Annabel Sturt."

"Oh yes. Annabel Sturt. That was a bad day. A very bad day. It started out well enough." He stops to take a sip of water then sits back in his chair, lacing his hands together on the table. "We struck a new line of oil so my men were happy and so was I. Not that I needed any more money. But it was from the satisfaction of the thing, you know. Then, as I was standing there watching the oil gush, I remembered something. Twenty years earlier to the day my mother had died. In an instant my happiness turned to anger. Not because I was sad she was dead, but because I hated the fact that she had ever lived. Now I know I've told you this before, Amelia, but I'll tell you again— Vernita Hawkins was a very bad woman. She did many things to me I do not want to speak of here but one of the worst things she did was abandoning me at my uncle's farm. Because of her, I spent my childhood being beaten and abused by that good-for-nothing son-of-a-bitch. I was nothing more than a punching bag to him.

"So that day when we struck the new line, I get to thinking over all the bad that was done to me, my lost childhood, and so on and so forth, and decide to take a drive to let off steam. To collect my thoughts, so to speak. I tell myself I'm not looking to cause anyone any harm. I'm just driving and that's all there is to it. And it had been a while since the last one. About a year or so, and to tell you the truth I was hoping that the worst of it was behind me. Then I happened upon Annabel Sturt. I had taken the truck to check on the perimeter fence in one of the fields that bordered the woods. There she was sitting on a rock eating tuna from a can. She was out for a day hike. I remember her well because she had this…" He gestures with his hand.

"Withered arm," I say.

He nods. "Yes, that's right, the arm. I remember thinking she must be plucky to do the hiking thing with a disability like that." He smiles, remembering. "When she sees me she says, 'Am I sure pleased to see you, mister. I've got myself terribly lost.' Like she was Dorothy from *The Wizard of Oz* or something." He pauses. "Sweet girl."

"What happened next?"

His face grows dark. "She was the first one I kept. It just happened. I felt the overwhelming need to hide us both away."

Hide her away, just like he did with me. I get a flash of being locked inside the trunk of his car with that terrifying hood over my head, and the long twisting roads that seemed to go on forever as he took me further and further away from civilization and into the woods.

55

"Did you sexually assault her?" I say.

"Yes."

"Multiple times?"

He exhales. "Yes."

"How long did you keep her for?"

"Three days."

"Where?"

"In one of the barns. Chained."

"Then what happened?"

"She tried to escape and I choked her. I thought of my mother when I did it."

"And where did you put her body?"

"In one of the disused wells."

"On your property?"

"Yes."

"Risky," says Novak.

Rex pauses and looks at him. "Yes, I've thought about that since. I think maybe part of me wanted to get caught."

"Or maybe you thought you could do anything you wanted and never face the consequences," states Novak.

I interject, wanting to avoid yesterday's tit-for-tat. "Is Annabel's body still there now?"

Rex pursues his lips. "I don't see why it wouldn't be."

I imagine Annabel Sturt's body in the well, the darkest of resting places, and feel my heart ache.

"Show us," says Novak, unraveling the map of the Hawkins refinery compound. There are wells all over the place, but Rex goes right too it.

"That one," he says. "Number twenty-three. It's spent. She'll be at the bottom."

Suddenly an alarm screeches above our heads and my heart leaps to my throat.

"What the hell is that?" says Novak.

Duane lets out a sigh and stands. "Lockdown. Probably a disturbance with one of the inmates." Outside three guards in riot gear run by with guns. "It happens sometimes. It can be a real zoo in here. Like I said—monkeys. Sorry, but I gotta get this guy back to his cell, and I'm afraid it means you folks need to evacuate, too."

"Evacuate? But we're in the middle of a plea agreement interview," I protest.

"And what about our recording equipment?" says March. "We can't just leave it unattended."

I look at Duane. "She's right. We need to preserve the chain of evidence."

Duane gives me a sincere look. "I understand, ma'am. Don't you worry yourself about that. Once I lock this door, no one will get back in. I'll make sure of it personally."

I pause, wondering if I should push things further.

"Ma'am?" says Duane, gesturing toward the door. "Someone will meet you all at the end of the corridor and escort you to the exit."

The siren rages above my head. Finally I pick up my bag and go.

"I would fuck her. Even with the baby. Hell, it's a turn-on when you think about it. Fucking a chick with another man's kid inside her…"

Rex glances at the guard. Duane Sheldon is his name. Bottom-feeder. Mouth-breather. All-around loser in life. They are walking along the corridor back to the cells for lockdown. It's slow going because of the ankle chains but Duane doesn't seem to mind as he plods alongside Rex, eyes glazed over and fixed on some midpoint in the distance. It's coming off him in waves, his pornographic lust. The thought of him—this ham-fisted, oafish Neanderthal—getting aroused over Amelia makes Rex sick.

"Oh yeah, the things I would do to her…"

One more word out of this filthy son-of-a-bitch's mouth and he's dead.

Rex keeps his voice even. "She's a good woman, Duane. About to be a mother, too. It's not right to be talking about her in that way."

Duane looks at Rex, eyes narrowing.

Rex continues. "I would say it's unchristian, as a matter of fact."

Duane stares at him awhile longer, then nods slowly, contemplating. "No, Rex, you're right. It is unchristian. Pay me no mind. I'm just as horny as hell these days. Ever since Linda left me." He spits on the floor. "Goddamn bitch."

"I understand, Duane. A man has his needs."

They reach the door leading to Rex's wing. Duane pulls out his keys and removes the chains from around Rex's belly and ankles, then signals the guard in the glass-paneled observation unit to let them in. There's a buzz as the lock is released and Duane and Rex step through the door and into the inner sanctum of C Wing—a horseshoe of three floors of cells, all looking outward. On the ground floor there's a rec area with fixed seating, a ping-pong table, and a beat-up television. Empty now because of the lockdown.

Rex smells smoke. He glances up at the second level. Water drips across the walkway and down the steel barriers. It's coming from the third cell on the end, which lies empty now.

Rex and Duane cross the rec floor to Rex's cell. Stan Weebly is in there, bent over the top of the upturned milk crate that doubles as a table, studying Rex's hobby-in-progress, a ship-in-a-bottle. Pudgy with Coke-bottle glasses, an IQ south of 60, and pants hoisted up so high his cuffs are a good three inches shy of where they should be, Stan Weebly is thirty-four years old and as dim-witted as hell. But the boy is good-natured, and Rex doesn't mind him because of that, even if he does trail Rex around like a lovesick puppy.

"What are you doing, fuck-face?" demands Duane.

Stan jumps in fright. He looks from Duane to Rex, eyes bugging out of his skull like a spring peeper frog.

"I wasn't touching it."

Rex gives him a nod. "It's all right, Stan. I know you were just looking."

Duane jabs a finger in Stan's chest, forcing Stan to step backward until he's right up against the cinderblock wall.

"Stealing Rex's stuff, huh? That's a mandatory six-week stint in solitary."

Stan's eyes widen. "No, no I...I wouldn't do that. I would never steal from Rex. He's my friend."

Rex places a hand on Duane's shoulder. "It's all right, Duane. I trust him."

"You sure, Rex? I don't mind doing a little paperwork to write up this mother-raping ass-fuck."

Rex waves a hand. "It's fine. You got better things to do, I'm sure."

Duane shrugs. "Suit yourself, Rex." He turns to Stan and grabs his chin, squeezing hard. "If I catch you and your sticky fingers with another inmate's stuff again, there'll be consequences, got me?"

Stan nods. "Yes, sir."

After Duane is gone, Rex lowers himself on to his bed. "Pay him no attention, Stan, the man's a cocksucker of the highest order."

Stan snickers. "Yeah, he is."

Rex turns his attention to the ship-in-a-bottle, picking up the large magnifying glass and pair of tweezers lying close by.

"You're doing a real swell job with it, Rex," says Stan, crouching down to peer through the glass.

"Thank you, Stan."

"What are you waiting on now?"

"Toothpicks for the mast, and a glue gun. Can you get me a glue gun, Stan?"

Stan laughs. "Yeah, sure. Want a buzz saw while I'm at it?"

Rex pauses and looks at Stan. Sometimes the boy could surprise him with a good comeback. Rex should give him more credit.

"Funny, Stan. Real funny."

Stan looks pleased. "Maybe you could show me how to make one…you know, when you've got time?"

Rex studies a splinter in the hull. "Sure, Stan. Be glad to." He glances at the door. "What's with the lockdown?"

Stan blows out a breath and puts his hands on his hips. "Diego went nuts again. Set fire to his bed then threw shit at that asshole guard, Moreno." He grins. "Got him right in the face, too. It was nasty."

"I bet."

"You would never do a thing like that, would you, Rex?"

"That's correct, Stan. I would not."

There's a ting on the cell bars. Rex looks up to see Bruce Jones. Black. Mid-forties. Over six-foot-five. Daddy was a guard. Granddaddy, too.

"Hey, Rex."

Rex smiles and gets to his feet. "Hello, Bruce. You been off? Haven't seen you for a while."

Bruce pulls a face. "They put me on over at A Block near the forensic unit. You wouldn't believe the crazy shit that goes on over there. How's the interview with the Feds?"

"Oh, you know, as well as can be expected."

Bruce clucks his tongue in sympathy. "It must be tough going over old ground, dredging up past mistakes."

"Time to do the right thing, Bruce. I got the Lord on my side and they're getting what they need now. That's the important thing. How's Jackie and the kids?"

Bruce's face lights up at mention of his family. "Jackie just got a promotion at the hospital so she's a happy lady.

I haven't seen her much lately because of that. We're like ships in the night these past couple of weeks." Bruce nods over Rex's shoulder at the model. "Speaking of ships, you're doing a great job there. It's my boy Tom's birthday in a couple of weeks, I might get him one of those. He's going to be nine and I don't think he's ever seen a ship-in-a-bottle before. It's all about iPads and Xboxes these days. He's going be scratching his head, wondering how the hell you get the ship in there. He's not the smartest boy at the best of times. Takes after his mother," he says, chuckling.

"Any idea how long lockdown's for?"

Bruce's eyes drift up to the second tier. "You heard what happened?"

Stan hovers behind Rex's shoulder. "I told him."

Bruce shakes his head in disgust. "That filthy son-of-bitch, Diego. They got him in confinement now, but there's new protocols. If there's an incident like that, lockdown will continue for the rest of the day. They say it unsettles the other inmates, might give them ideas. All this new health and safety shit. Overkill in my opinion."

"In that case, would you do me a favor, Bruce? Would you make sure that Amelia Kellaway gets the message that we can get back to proceedings tomorrow? I don't want her waiting around if she doesn't have to."

"Sure. That I can do." Bruce looks over his shoulder. "I better go. Shouldn't really be out here given we're in lockdown but I wanted to see how it all went."

"Appreciate it, Bruce."

"Oh, hey, I nearly forgot." Bruce pulls a stack of letters from his back pocket. "More fan-mail." Bruce shakes his head, bemused. "These women crack me up. This time one of them even sent you her panties. Strictly speaking you shouldn't have those, but I'll let them through. I figure you won't be digging your way out of here with a pair of panties."

He passes the letters to Rex through the bars. "See you in a bit."

"Sure thing, Bruce. Thanks."

After he's gone, Rex glances down at the stack of letters in his hands. He'd never had any desire to read the so-called fan mail that began arriving the first day he came to Aken. Sent to him by females from all around the world. Females wanting to save his soul, offer companionship or sexual stimulation. He had absolutely no interest in women who lowered themselves to such a degree. It wasn't worth giving the letters to Stan either as it was wholly unlikely that Stan could read past a grade two level.

A patch of sheer peach-colored fabric protrudes from the top envelope. Rex pulls on it and withdraws a pair of lacy panties. Stan stares at the underwear hanging from the end of Rex's finger.

Rex holds them out. "They're all yours, Stan."

Stan hesitates.

"Go on, take them," insists Rex.

Stan accepts the panties and lifts them to his nose. "They've still got her scent on them."

Dumping the stack of letters in the drawer, Rex puts on his spectacles and sits down at his desk.

"What say we have quiet time now, Stan," he says, turning on the lamp.

Reaching to his right, he picks up the tweezers and white cotton thread and gets to work.

11

For the next three days, I try to maintain my composure as Rex continues with his account of the abductions and rapes and locations of the bodies. It sucks the air from the room. All the hurt and ruin and death and destruction. But I have to admit, it's fascinating. Novak, March, O'Leary, and I hang on his every word. Listening with intense concentration. Feeling it all. Caught in a state of hyperarousal that is at once both strangely energizing and overwhelmingly draining.

I study him closely. Watching for any signs of sincerity and remorse. And they're all there. The solemn intonation. The right sad face at the right sad time. An appropriate apologetic gesture. The chained hand levitating over the bible. Water filling his downcast eyes.

Yes, all the signs that he is sorry are there, but are they genuine? And do I want them to be genuine? Because if they are, what is it that really separates him from me?

There's a clear pattern to his offending. Befriend. Abduct. Rape. Kill. I don't know what the worst part is— the rape and murder, or knowing that a human being who pretends to be your friend could betray you so deeply. Because that's what I remember the most, his betrayal and my own deep sense of foolishness at myself for believing he was simply a friendly stranger.

"I admit, Amelia, that by that point I was out of control."

Rex glances down at the two photographs of Agnes Olofsson and Heidi Sandström, a pair of young Swedish tourists trekking a little-known route in Silver Creek Falls.

The two who came directly after me. The final two victims according to Rex. By that stage, Rex had been on the run from police and hiding out in the woods. After encountering the two women, he had tied Heidi to a tree and forced her to watch him strangle Agnes to death, after which he killed Heidi.

He swallows and looks down at his hands. "I know it was a truly terrible thing to do."

"How did you dispose of their belongings?" I ask.

He looks thoughtful. "They didn't have much, if I remember rightly, just a day pack each. One was black and the other one was red. There's a lake there, near the falls, so I threw the packs into that. It's funny, I remember thinking right after I hurled the packs into the water that I had made a terrible mistake by not weighing them down with rocks or some such thing. But as I stood watching, they sank to the bottom almost immediately."

"And the bodies?" I ask. "Did you put them in the water, too?"

Rex shakes his head. "I buried them a stone's throw from the lake."

"Separately?"

He shakes his head again. "Together. It was easier that way."

Digging two graves was too much effort for him. I try not to let the disgust show on my face. "Can you indicate on the map for us, please, Rex?"

He studies the map and traces an inland route with his forefinger, then taps a spot called Lotus Rock.

"It was around there somewhere," he says, making a cross with the pen. "There's a slight plateau with a bunch of boulders that overlooks the forest. At that time, there was also a stand of trees nearby—firs, I think. I'm pretty sure that's where the grave is."

"Pretty sure?" says Novak. "You need to be more precise than that."

Rex studies the map again. Eventually, he shakes his head and sits back. "I'm sorry. You'll need dogs."

Novak narrows his eyes. "You better not be shitting us, Hawkins."

"Why would I do that?"

"How come you can remember where you put every other victim accept these ones?"

Rex scratches his cheekbone. "Like I said before, things were well out of control by that point. I was on the run and I had a lot on my mind so my memory is a touch jumbled on the subject." He nods toward the map. "That's the very best I can do."

"Sure it is," says Novak, sarcastically.

O'Leary exhales. "My client has given you his answer, Special Agent Novak. Can we move on please? In fact," he says, looking down at his notes, "I do believe that we have come to the end of Rex's account of all the murders. Is that correct, Rex?"

Rex nods. "It is indeed, Victor." Rex looks at me. "I've told everything I know about all of the women, Amelia. I've laid out all the wrong I've done bare and held not one iota back, I promise you. I hope it brings some peace, I really do, and I'm happy to answer any follow-up questions you may have."

I don't say anything, instead letting my eyes drift to the wall over Rex's shoulder. Just above the radiator, there's a poster about living with HIV. To the left of that, someone has etched the word REVENGE into the wall in nasty sharp capitals. O'Leary clears his throat and looks at me. I suspect he's waiting for the formal wrap-up spiel for the recording.

March meets my eyes. I look away, suddenly afraid. My throat tightens and I think I might be sick. I reach down to my satchel and withdraw the file.

"I'm not trying to catch you out, Rex," I say, placing the file on the table. "I wanted to give you a chance to tell us everything first."

Rex's eyes don't leave my face. "And I have, Amelia. I promise you."

I hold his gaze. "Are you sure about that, Rex?"

He stares at me and says nothing.

O'Leary shifts in his seat. "What is this, Amelia?"

I open the file and take out the photo of the little girl and place it on the table in front of Rex. Cindy McDonald. Nine years old.

"Is this where it started, Rex?" I say. "Cindy McDonald?"

His eyes drop to the photo. "I've never seen her before."

"Take another look."

Rex lifts his eyes. "I don't know how much clearer I can be, Amelia—I do not know this person."

I glance down at my notes. "Cindy's body was found in scrubland with bruises around her neck. The autopsy showed that her hymen was torn and she'd endured a vicious prolonged sexual assault."

Rex pushes the photo away. "That's disgusting. I would never do such a thing."

"Cindy lived on the farm not far from your property. I believe you would have been sixteen at the time."

He shakes his head, adamant. "I wouldn't, not a child, Amelia, not a little girl."

"Cindy went out to the henhouse to collect eggs, just like she did every morning right before school, but on that particular day she never came back."

He stares at me. "You're not listening, Amelia. I am not capable of such a thing."

O'Leary shakes his head, exasperated. "This is totally out of order, Amelia, ambushing my client like this." He turns to Rex. "Don't say anything else."

I ignore O'Leary and pull a written statement from the file.

"There was a witness, Rex. A mailman. Hank Barker. He said he saw a youth fitting your description walking down the road with Cindy. He assumed you were brother and sister."

O'Leary scoffs. "I'm sure Rex couldn't have been the only teenage male in the area."

I carry on, pulling out a newspaper clipping. "And then there's this."

It's a large front page spread of the search for Cindy, including a photograph of the search party being briefed by police.

"The entire community turned out. Searched day and night for four days until they found Cindy's body in scrubland." I tap the photo. "That looks a lot like you, don't you think?"

Rex keeps his eyes focused on me.

I soften my voice. "Go on, Rex. Take a look."

He lowers his eyes and skims the photo. He frowns.

"That's you, isn't it?" I say.

Eyes still on the image, he says, "I accept that it does bear a resemblance. But I can't say I ever remember being there and I certainly don't remember anything about any missing girl."

"But you were neighbors?"

"You don't need to answer that," says O'Leary.

Rex holds up his hand. "It's all right, Vic. If Amelia says we were neighbors then I accept that we were. Things were difficult for me at that time. My mother had not long left me at my uncle's. The abuse was bad. I try not to think about that period in my life."

"Cindy's parents died never knowing the truth, but she has a sister who needs some peace. You could give her that peace, Rex. You could tell her what happened."

He shakes his head. "I don't know anything, Amelia."

I pause. "Maybe you didn't mean to."

He raises his eyes to the ceiling. "No."

"Maybe things got out of hand."

He swings his head from side-to-side. "No, no, no. I just wouldn't do that."

"Oh, cut the bullshit, Hawkins," snaps Novak. "You're as guilty as sin."

Rex exhales. "Listen, I don't know how many times I have to say this—I did not do anything to any little girl."

Novak stabs the table with his index finger. "Do I need to remind you that if we find you've committed a crime that you haven't confessed to during this interview, you're looking at the death penalty?"

Rex stares at him. "I've told you everything I know."

Novak lowers his voice. "You still think about her, don't you? At night, when you're alone. You see her in front of you, feel her neck in your hands."

O'Leary speaks. "That's enough."

Novak ignores him. "I bet you still have wet dreams about poor little Cindy."

Rex glares at Novak. "You're sick."

"Oh, I'm the sick one?"

O'Leary turns to me. "Amelia, are you really going to allow this?"

But I'm not about to interfere.

"You sickos are all the same," Novak continues, shaking his head at the ceiling. "You think you're all so fucking clever."

Rex crosses his arms. "I've told you the truth."

Novak rises out of his chair, looming over Rex. "But you're not clever at all. You're just an animal who likes raping little girls."

O'Leary slams his folder shut and stands. "That's it— interview over."

Novak glowers at Rex. "Did she cry, Hawkins? Did she plead for her life? Did she scream when you raped her and tore her apart?"

Rex smashes his fist on the table and leaps to his feet. "Shut your nasty mouth!"

We stare at him in stunned silence. He stands there, breathing.

"I've told you everything I know," he says, finally. "Absolutely everything. There's nothing more to tell."

He glances at March and frowns. I turn to look. Blood is dripping from her nose.

"Oh, for Christ's sake, March," says Novak.

March raises her fingertips to her nostrils and sees the blood.

"Sorry, sorry," she says, scraping her chair back and getting to her feet.

"Someone get the woman a goddamn tissue," growls Novak.

"I'm okay," she says, pinching the bridge of her nose. March stops at the door. "Sorry, Ms. Kellaway, you'll need to pause the recording."

"That won't be necessary," says O'Leary, fuming. "We're done here."

I glance at Rex. His face is a blank, inscrutable wall.

"Yes, Victor," I say. "I think we are."

12

It's after midnight by the time we hit New York City and another forty minutes before we pull up outside my apartment. Novak cuts the engine and the three of us sit there in silence. The street is empty, apart from a woman wearing earmuffs walking a French bulldog with a pink scarf coiled round its stubby neck. She shouldn't be walking alone at night. Not a woman on her own.

It makes me think of Cindy McDonald. We will never get justice for her now. Not without a confession from Rex. There was simply no evidence. Nothing physical, barely anything circumstantial, either. Nothing that would stand up in court anyway.

It was Jane Duffy who made us look. "There'll be a first, some time ago, in his younger years. A sloppy killing with mistakes that won't seem like his work at all. Tortured animals before that. There are always animals. That's the first sign. Testing pain on living things. Testing his own reactions to that. Then comes the first human victim, typically a child or elderly person. Someone defenseless."

So March and I searched the records for anything that fit. We went back to his early days at the farm. We looked for unsolved murders in the community around that time. There was an old woman bashed to death in her bed. A vagrant found strangled in some bushes behind the local school. A missing toddler who was thought to have possibly wandered off into a lake and drowned. Then we came across the newspaper clippings of the search for Cindy McDonald and everything fell into place.

When I went to interview Cindy's sister, Fiona, a quiet woman in her mid-fifties, she told me how her mother would pray every night for Cindy's lost soul and how her father never once said Cindy's name after she was murdered. "They both died of grief," Fiona had said.

Now I couldn't bring Fiona any peace, either. Even after I promised her I would.

"What time's your flight?" I say, staring out my window.

March tips her wrist to glance at her watch. "Just over three hours."

"You two, I could never have done this without your help," I say.

Novak looks at me. "You're welcome. Though sometimes I wonder if I should think about getting into another line of work. Like pizza delivery."

"Keep me posted on how the body recovery goes?"

He nods. "We'll make sure you get real-time updates, won't we, March?"

"Yes, sir."

"I wish I could be there."

Novak raises his eyebrows in amusement. "We can't very well have a pregnant woman waddling around on a crime scene now can we?"

I give him a smile. "No, I suppose not."

I recall the heated discussion Ethan and I had a few months ago when Ethan argued bitterly against me taking part in the body recovery. Eventually, I agreed not to go. But sitting on the sidelines is going to be excruciating.

"You guys have a big job ahead," I say.

Novak rubs the stubble on his chin. "Ain't that the truth."

73

I look at March. "Laura, you'll send me the digital copies of the interviews so I can get started on the statement of facts?"

She nods. "I'll get them to you tomorrow."

I pat her arm. "Not tomorrow. Take a break for the weekend. Monday is fine."

*

Novak helps me bring my files and overnight bag into the apartment. Ethan is asleep on the couch when we enter, remnants of a microwave chili dinner hardening on the coffee table in front of him, the TV quietly showing an ice hockey game. We tread carefully so as not to wake him and whisper our goodbyes.

After Novak departs, I head over to the sofa and look down at Ethan. Such a beautiful man. Such a kind and gentle soul. He'll make a wonderful father. The antithesis to Rex Hawkins and his murderous and deranged heart.

My monitor beeps. I hurry to silence it, but it's too late. Ethan's eyes flutter open.

"Hey," he says, sleepily. "You were going to text me."

I smile. "I did." I scoot next to him and wrap my arms around his waist and sink into a hug. "God, you feel like home."

"Was that your heart monitor?" he says, kissing the top of my head.

"Too much caffeine."

We lapse into silence. I feel the thud of his heart beneath my cheekbone.

Eventually, he says, "So?"

"So?" I sigh.

"How did it go?"

I close my eyes. "Do we have to talk about it?"

"Not if you don't want to."

"God, I'm tired."

I feel him there, alert. Listening.

Finally, I give in. "He told us everything. About every last one of them. All except for Cindy McDonald."

"Well done," he says. I stiffen and he must feel it because he adds, "I'm sure you did everything you could about Cindy."

"It was like he didn't want to admit it to himself. He kept saying, 'Not a little girl. I wouldn't hurt a little girl.'"

"You sound like you feel sorry for him."

I balk. "Well, I'm not. He's a bastard. A pathetic bastard."

Ethan pauses. "So, that's it then? It's over? Your part?"

I nod. "Just typing up the statement of facts."

I don't tell him about the real-time updates of the body recovery.

"I can focus on you and the baby now," I say.

I feel Ethan relax and I'm pleased. He sits up and looks at me, eyes twinkling.

"What is it?" I say.

He takes my hand. "I want to show you something."

"Show me what?"

"I was going to do it in the morning, but what the hell."

He leads me up the hallway into the spare room. He opens the door with a flourish and turns on the light.

"Ta-da!"

The entire room is pink and white. The antique bassinet we found on Craigslist has been painted a soft shade of alabaster, and hanging above that is a pretty mobile of the solar system with all the planets gently aglow. A huge pile of soft toys is stacked neatly in the corner—obligatory teddy bears, puppies, cats, and even a T-Rex dinosaur—and next to that, the IKEA change table and set of drawers we bought months ago sit perfectly assembled.

"Ethan, this must have taken you forever."

"Do you like it?"

I plant a kiss on his cheek. "It's beautiful." I glance around, touching the fleecy blanket in the bassinet. "Everything looks perfect."

He looks around. "I wanted it to be a surprise."

"And it is. It's a wonderful surprise."

We stand staring at the room.

"God, Amelia, we are going to have a baby."

13

The body recovery is going to be a massive undertaking. Novak walked me through the logistics a few weeks earlier. He and a team of five other agents have been working closely with the specialist crews involved in Sandy Hook and the 2017 Las Vegas shootings. Together they developed a comprehensive plan, specifically in relation to the management and processing of multiple bodies at once. Two critical factors had to be taken into account—establishing identification and cause of death. Establishing cause of death is particularly important as we do not want Rex Hawkins crying foul in a few years' time that his confession had been coerced and that some or all of the victims had died of natural causes as opposed to his own hands.

A refrigerator truck and a giant cool store have been hired to transport and hold the bodies. Three medical examiners will perform their duties in the cool store, determining cause of death and victim identification by comparing DNA samples taken from relatives. To that end, a temporary lab has also been established to conduct the DNA analysis as quickly as possible, which means no waiting around for weeks to find out if there is a match or not.

To minimize stress for the families and speed up the return of the bodies of their sisters and daughters, the plan is to work as efficiently and quickly as possible. But no one is under any illusions: in some cases, there is unlikely to be much left of the remains. Bones if we're lucky. But anything is better than nothing as far as the families are concerned—every single of them had told me so.

When I wake up on Monday morning, my first thoughts turn to the search and recovery. They will be out in force today, combing the woods. Starting just west of Ashland, in southern Oregon, they'll gradually make their way north, Novak and March at the forefront. I feel a stab of something. Envy? I lie there and stare at the ceiling. Don't be stupid, I tell myself. I have a good life. A husband who loves me. A baby on the way. Other women would long to be in my position. Still, I can't shake it. The thought that who I am is about to disappear in a cloud of diapers and 2 a.m. wake-up calls.

I work on the statement of facts until lunchtime, then check the online news. All the notable sites have exploded. CNN. Fox. Even the BBC. The first body has been recovered. It is suspected to be Samantha Logan, twenty-three, missing since 1998. There's footage of her elderly parents weeping and hugging each other outside their local church, followed by a long shot of two police officers emerging from the forest with a black body bag. I feel a twinge. So much for the real-time updates from Novak.

Suddenly my own face flashes up on screen. It's a photograph of me taken several years ago leaving the hospital, limping across the parking lot with my new cane and first pair of specially adjusted orthopedic shoes. I'm shocked by how frail and vulnerable I look.

"…and this is the woman responsible for bring this evil predator to justice. Assistant District Attorney Amelia Kellaway, herself a victim of the depraved monster. Ms. Kellaway secured the plea deal with Rex Hawkins in which he agreed to provide details of all the murders and locations of the bodies in return for the State of Oregon not pursing the death penalty."

More recent footage of me in downtown Manhattan appears. I'm emerging from the courthouse deep in conversation with John Liber, my baby bump clearly showing. It must have been taken a few months back. I didn't even know the camera was there.

I feel myself go hot. I hate this. Being on display like a carnival attraction. But that's what all of us are now, aren't we, his victims? The objects of the other people's morbid curiosity.

I turn away from screen and go make a coffee. Then I get back to work.

*

I'm still in front of my laptop working on the statement of facts when Ethan gets home.

He kisses the top of my head and glances at the screen. "I thought you'd be watching the coverage."

I shrug. "I had work to do."

He takes off his jacket and puts it on the back of the chair. "They're playing it everywhere. This afternoon I caught the subway downtown and people were even watching it on their phones," he says. "They've recovered two bodies, and trying for a third tonight." He kisses my head again. "Have you eaten?"

"I'm not hungry."

He frowns. "You had lunch today though?"

"A smoothie. Kale. Blueberries." I pull a face.

He reaches over and shuts my laptop. "Then what you need, my love, is some good old-fashioned meat and three vegetables."

Ethan cooks us a nice meal. Fillet steak in mushroom sauce with green beans and mashed potatoes. Iron is good for the baby, he tells me as we sit at the kitchen table across from each other. He has even lit a candle and I watch it now, flickering under the stream of the heat pump.

"You're quiet," he says.

I stab at my beans. "Just tired."

"How's the steak?"

"Good. Perfect. As always." I give him a smile.

He puts down his fork and looks at me. "What is it?"

"Nothing."

"Amelia."

I don't say anything.

He gives me a sympathetic look. "I know it must be hard, not being part of the action, but you know you can't be there."

I choose my words carefully. "Ethan, I've been thinking. I know I said I'd take the first year off…"

He sits back in his chair and stares at me. "You can't be serious."

"Ethan."

He gets to his feet, picks up our dinner plates, and takes them to the sink.

"A baby needs its mother," he says, jaw firmly set.

"We can get good help."

He drops the cutlery into the sink with a clang and turns on the faucet. "We talked about this before. We agreed you would stay home for the first year. My mom was there for me when I was little, and I want the same for my kids. We've saved for it. Everything's in place."

"I can't be an effective mother without my own identity."

80

He continues with the dishes without looking at me. "What the hell are you talking about—you'll still have an identity."

"I need to work, Ethan."

"Our baby is more important than work," he says.

I shake my head, exasperated. "Don't be so dramatic. I'm not talking about giving her up for adoption. I'll take the first four weeks off, go back to work after that. A lot of women do it."

"It sounds like you've got this all planned out."

"It's not 1958, Ethan. I need to have a life, too."

"You will have a life. You'll be a mother. What could be more important than that?"

"Ethan, be reasonable."

He turns and looks at me. "Do you even want this baby?"

I pause, hurt. "How could you even say that?"

He sighs. "Sorry. I didn't mean that."

I stand up.

He frowns. "Hey, where are you going? We should talk about this."

"I need a bath," I say, without looking back.

14

I hurry up 2nd Avenue toward midtown, doing my best to avoid the treacherous slush puddles and mountain of garbage bags piled along the sidewalk. It's a clear blue day, but the wind is arctic, which makes the temperature seem more like seventeen below zero than the forty registering on my phone. In wintry conditions like these, it's hard with the cane because I'm liable to take a tumble if I'm not especially careful, something I can do without at the moment. My ears are burning, too, and I chide myself for not wearing a beanie.

Ethan left this morning without saying goodbye. I was surprised by his childishness. Surprised and hurt. This isn't easy. This motherhood thing. He has no idea what it's like having something tethered to your insides. Having your entire life about to change. The sacrifice involved. It's easy for him. He can carry on as normal. Go to work. Be out in the world. Reach his potential. Me on the other hand, well, I'm expected to stay at home, be the good mom, the best wife, no questions asked.

Tears sting. I hate fighting with Ethan. It makes me feel small and alone and selfish and mean. I reach the door to Dr. Liu's consulting rooms and pause on the steps to wipe my tears with the thumb of my glove.

"You okay, sweetheart?"

I look up. It's a woman with a very red nose and a frown on her face dressed head-to-toe in Lululemon, probably on her way to Central Park for a workout. The woman has taken out her ear bud to talk to me and the faint strain of "Single Ladies" by Beyoncé wafts between us.

"I'm good," I say.

Her frown deepens. "You sure? You don't look it."

I squint up the sky. "Can you believe this cold?"

The woman relaxes a little and looks around. "Yeah. It's brutal."

"Thanks for stopping, but I'm okay. Really."

I give her a smile. Satisfied I'm not about to throw myself headlong into traffic, she wishes me a good day, pops her ear bud back in, and carries on her way. I watch her leave, slightly envious of the bounce in her step. It had been a long time since I had anything close to a bounce in mine.

Resting my hand on my cane, I turn and enter the door of the brownstone and take the lift to the second-floor consulting rooms that Dr. Sandy Liu shares with three other OB/GYNs. I glance around the plush waiting area at the other expectant mothers seated there. They all look so calm and serene, pleasant expressions fixed to their faces as they skim the latest *House and Garden*. One has brought along what must be her husband or partner, and they sit together on the contemporary mid-century sofa, arms locked, sharing a copy of *Martha Stewart Living*. I feel the sudden weight of guilt. Ethan doesn't even know I'm here.

I don't feel like running the gamut of the same tired old questions—boy or girl? when are you due? picked out a name yet?—so I take the seat in the corner and check the latest progress of the body recovery on my phone.

"Amelia?"

I look up and see Sandy standing in the doorway. Hauling myself to my feet, I follow her down the hallway.

Walking behind her, I'd forgotten how beautiful she is. Porcelain skin that looks like it has never seen a full day of sun, sleek black hair tied in a ponytail at the nape of a slender neck, graceful deportment of someone who's spent years doing ballet or yoga or both.

After we take a seat in her office, she says, "So how are you?"

"I've been better."

I run through my list of things: Nausea. Unpredictable heart monitor. Cramps. She nods, listening. I leave out the part about the argument with Ethan and my lousy expectant mother attitude.

When I finish, Sandy rises from her chair. "Let's take a look, shall we?"

I get up and lie on the gurney and pull up my shirt. Sandy's soft hands roam my abdomen, the sleeve of her blue, feather-light cashmere sweater grazing my skin. She turns on the ultrasound and lowers the lights.

"This might be cold," she says, squirting a blob of gel on my stomach.

She glides the transducer probe back and forth, eyes fixed to the monitor. I look too and see the shape of my little girl, tucked into herself, fingers splaying sporadically as if she's waving at me. I'd had a first-trimester ultrasound at twelve weeks, but this is a whole different story. I stare in wonderment. I can see everything. Her fingers and toes. Her limbs and knees and feet. Her tiny, fully formed human face. Everything is so clear yet so ghostly.

The sound of her heartbeat pounds around the room. Whoa. Whoa. Whoa. I feel my eyes water. My baby. God. I can't really believe it. I think of Ethan. He would have loved to have seen this.

84

Sandy's eyes shift to my face. She places her hand on my shoulder.

"You okay?"

I nod, biting my lip to stop the tears. "Is everything all right? I mean is she healthy?"

Sandy nods. "Everything looks good." She leans over and hangs the transducer probe back on its hook. "Why don't you get dressed and we'll talk at my desk."

By the time I slip my clothes back on and take a seat, Sandy's scrolling through her tablet examining the data from my heart monitor. She turns to me, lacing her fingers in her lap. "First the good news," she says. "The baby appears healthy. She's developing normally. Heartbeat is strong. I have no concerns about her at this stage."

I feel a wave of relief wash over me. "And the bad news?"

Sandy frowns. "The cramps are a puzzle. They're not Braxton Hicks. A common cause of cramping can be round ligament pain. The round ligament is a muscle that supports the uterus, and when it stretches, you may feel a sharp, stabbing pain, or a dull ache in your lower abdomen. I suspect that's what's been happening."

She pauses.

"What is it?" I say.

She glances at her computer and clicks on a page with a graph on it. "Your blood pressure is still of concern." She pivots the screen to show me. I see the graph of sharp up and down lines like a polygraph exam. "It's all over the place, quite frankly. I'll order a urine sample and bloods to screen for preeclampsia, but given the baby's within healthy weight range, it's unlikely to be that. I prefer not to give you blood pressure medication if I can help it." She looks at me directly. "How's your emotional state?"

I swallow. "Fine."

"Having a baby is a major life change. It can be overwhelming for some women."

I feel myself bristle. "There's nothing wrong with my mental faculties, Sandy."

She nods and moves on smoothly. "And you're still working?"

"Things are tapering off." I hear the defensive note in my voice and hate myself for it.

Sandy pauses. "Amelia, I see a lot of driven, professional women in here. It's hard for them to adjust during late-term pregnancy. You're not alone. It doesn't make you a bad person or a bad mother—it makes you human. Look, the short point is, you need to take it easy. For you and the baby. Try some prenatal yoga or swimming or massage. You should be enjoying this time, you'll never get it back."

I look down at my hands. "Are you saying I might be putting the baby under stress?"

"Potentially."

That's hard to hear. I don't want to harm my baby.

"Listen, everything's okay right now," says Sandy. "But as you get closer to delivery, certain risk factors increase. You just need to be more mindful of your approach."

I nod. "I understand. I'll do better."

"Good."

Sandy turns to her computer, taps a few keys, and the printer bursts into life. She hands me the image of today's ultrasound. I look down and trace my finger around that little waving hand.

"She's beautiful, isn't she?" I say.

"She most certainly is. Let's make her entry into the world as smooth as possible."

*

I stop at the supermarket on the way home from the clinic. I want to make Ethan's favorite dinner—lasagna and garlic bread. I want to apologize for being so difficult. I want to tell him that I love him and that I will keep my promise and take the first year off, work be damned. I want to tell him that he and the baby are the most important things to me.

I'm in the middle aisle reaching for a can of Roma tomatoes when I get a call from Novak.

"He played us, Amelia."

It takes me a moment to shift gears. "What do you mean? Who played us?"

"Rebecca Kilmore's body isn't here."

I exhale. "Oh."

"Yeah."

A woman with a boy in a stroller stops close by and studies the rows of eggs. I lower my voice and turn my head.

"Maybe he just got it wrong. It's been years, after all. The landscape changes. It could be an honest mistake."

"Then how do you explain Bernetta James and Caitlyn McLellan?"

My hand grips the trolley. "Jesus. They weren't where he said they were either?"

"Got it in one."

"But why would he do that? He's got nothing to gain from lying."

"Don't ask me how that son-of-a-bitch's mind works," says Novak.

I watch as the mom with the stroller reaches for a carton of eggs and they slip from her grasp and crash all over the floor. The little boy starts laughing and clapping his hands.

"Am I interrupting something?" says Novak.

I glance at the smashed eggs. "Grocery store drama."

Thankfully a store employee is close by and goes to help. I discreetly wheel my cart a little further along.

"Have you told the families anything?" I ask.

"Not yet."

"Good. Let me talk to O'Leary first and find out what's going on."

I hear Novak breathe through the phone. "Make it quick, Amelia. The media's starting to get antsy. It won't be long before they put two and two together."

I leave my cart right where it is and go make the call.

15

It's rec time in C Block and the usual hullabaloo is going on outside Rex's cell. Earlier there'd been an exchange of words over a card game and another one over chess. The matter had been settled when Ramirez threw a cup of boiling Ramen noodles over his competitor, a nineteen-year-old kid called Bucky Billy, so named because of his badly protruding two front teeth.

At the time, Rex chuckled to himself. No such thing as good sportsmanship in here. It was every man for himself. Especially as far as gambling away your stash of marijuana or cigarettes or coveted cell phone was concerned.

Rex lifts the magnifying glass to eyeline and examines the slither of wood he'd managed to salvage from the workshop. Balsa wood would have been preferable but beggars can't be choosers and he can live with this alternative. It is as light as balsa although not as hard, but the more important thing was that he'd managed to pocket a square of sandpaper discarded on the shop-room floor so he could shape the wood exactly the way he wanted regardless of what type it was. Sure, the sandpaper was a coarser grit size than he would have liked—a fine three-hundred-point grit would have been optimal—but he would make do with this and he was grateful for the find. It is a wonder how opportunities place themselves before him like that. Sometimes he feels so goddamn lucky to be alive.

His eyes drift down to the sketch of the hull laid out in front of him. He compares the would-be left side of the hull he holds in his fingertips with the image on the paper. Just a little more sanding on the tip and it will be ready to join with the other four components he'd sanded into shape earlier. Then comes the fun part. The part that requires a hand as steady as a surgeon's and the patience of a saint. When he will get to guide the different parts of the hull through the neck of the bottle with a pair of tweezers and glue them together one at a time. The glue is not genuine glue, of course, because inmates would use that to get high. Instead Rex mixed flour with water and used that as a substitute. So far the flour glue has stuck well on all the other parts of the ship's construction, like the boom and the keel, and he is hoping the same will be said for the hull.

"Hey, Rex." Rex glances up to see Stan in the doorway. "They're giving an update on the body recovery on the TV."

Rex turns back to his slither of wood. "Is that a fact, Stan."

The body recovery has been running on the rec room TV all week. Rex isn't sure what the fuss is about. For the most part, he'd rather not have had the attention at all.

Stan glances over his shoulder. "They had some really good drone footage a minute ago. You could see right into the grave where they were digging."

Rex wipes his hand on a rag and gets to his feet. He looks out his cell door. More than a dozen men are gathered around the TV.

Stan grins. "You're a big star."

"I don't know about that, Stan."

"They're calling you the Oregon oil rig killer."

"Well, that's just silly, Stan, the Hawkins refinery isn't even in Oregon."

"One of them profilers said you committed over a hundred murders," says Stan, eyes lighting up.

"I wouldn't believe everything you hear."

Stan frowns, thinking. "Maybe that's part of my problem, Rex. Maybe I always believe too much about what other people say and that gets me into trouble."

"You're fine just the way you are, Stan."

Rex returns to his desk and picks up the piece of hull. He looks at it closely. "How many bodies do they say they got so far?"

"Five, I think."

Just then Knepper, a big, ugly, God-awful hulk of an animal with a homemade tattoo of a Nazi swastika between his cold black eyes appears.

He shoves Stan out of the way. "Move, motherfucker."

"What do you want, Knepper?" says Rex, not looking up.

Knepper nods toward the rec room. "Suppose you think this makes you some kind of Mr. Big? A real life come as you are serial killer?" He crosses his arms. "I'm impressed. Really I am."

"They say Rex killed over a hundred women," says Stan.

Knepper glares at Stan. "Fuck up, retard. No one's talking to you."

Rex frowns. "There's no need for that, Knepper."

Knepper snorts. "Or what, Hawkins? You gonna put those tiny fucking hands around this?" He thrusts out his tree-trunk of a neck.

Rex says nothing.

"Yeah. Thought so," says Knepper. "Not such a tough guy in here, are you?" He wanders around the cell, taking his time. He looks at the ship. "Aren't you a bit old to be playing with toys?"

"It's not a toy," says Stan, defensively. "Rex is a craftsman."

Knepper pivots and shoves a finger in Stan's face. "I thought I told you to shut up. You got shit in your ears as well as your brain?"

Rex puts down the piece of wood and looks at Knepper. "Haven't you something better to do? Or is picking on someone weaker than yourself how you get your kicks?"

Knepper sneers. "I don't know how you can defend this cocksucker. You do know this retard slit his mother's throat and threw her off a bridge? But not before raping every single one of her orifices. What kind of sick motherfucker does that?" He taps Stan's forehead. "Did you get that joke, retard? I called you a motherfucker because you are a motherfucker."

Stan's mouth twitches. Rex can tell he's holding back tears.

"How's Larry boy these days?" says Rex.

Knepper stares at Rex. "Larry boy is none of your fucking business."

"You know, it would be a real shame if Larry boy found himself in solitary, wouldn't it? For, say, I don't know, six months? What do you think that would do to him? What do you think that would do to you?"

A flash of concern crosses Knepper's face. "Leave Larry boy out of this."

"You know I got friends in high places," continues Rex. "It would be a sad thing for a man to be without his companion. I think we can both agree on that, can't we, Knepper?"

Knepper hands briefly clench at his side.

Rex nods toward the cell door. "You best leave us be."

Knepper wavers, glancing at the cell door.

"Go on. Get," says Rex.

Eventually, Knepper heads toward the door. He pauses there. "Don't think this means you aren't on my list, Hawkins."

"Let's call it a draw," says Rex.

Knepper throws Rex an icy stare and departs, but not before issuing a snarl in Stan's direction.

After he's gone, Stan says, "Faggot."

"Pass me those tweezers, would you, Stan?"

Stan hands Rex the tweezers and Rex uses them to cinch the wood and carefully guide it through the neck of the bottle. Next, he picks up the miniature paintbrush and applies the flour glue to the edge of the wood and fixes it into place with the rest of the hull. He sits back and smiles. It's always the smallest things that give the greatest pleasure, isn't it?

16

I hang up the phone from O'Leary and look around the room. Disappointment washes over me. Disappointment in myself. Disappointment in Rex. Disappointment for the families. I should have expected this. For things not to go smoothly. For things to go downhill. Stupidly, I had believed that the worst part was over. That the hardest thing was facing Rex and getting it all down and written up and signed. I couldn't have been more wrong.

I wait a few minutes to gather my thoughts before I phone Novak. I watch the hands of the Mickey Mouse clock on the middle shelf of the bookcase. A vintage copper clock with a slight patina that Ethan and I had found in a dusty old antique shop in Nantucket. The glass face is broken so the little gloved hands are exposed. I watch those gloved hands now, as they tick around an entire four rotations before I finally punch in Novak's number.

He answers immediately. "So what'd he say?" I hear voices in the background. Wind through treetops. He must still be out on location.

"He needs to see the locations with his own eyes."

There's a stunned pause. "Hawkins wants to come to Oregon? So the motherfucker can escape? How dumb does he think we are? That's totally out of the fucking question."

"I know."

"Besides, that was ruled out in the early plea discussions. We made that very clear."

"I know."

"The Oregon governor will never go for it."

I exhale. "I know."

The governor, Sheila Brenton. A right wing, tough on crime, root out corruption kind of gal. When we first briefed her about the case, she'd refused to give her consent to the plea agreement. In fact, she'd tapped her pen against her lip and said, "Well, I've never seen a son-of-a-bitch more deserving of the death penalty. I would lift the moratorium for this." It took a lot of convincing to sway her from that type of thinking.

"The problem is one of evidence, ma'am," I had said. "Quite frankly, we're short on it. There's no DNA. No hairs. No fibers. Nothing to tie him to the killings. It's all just circumstantial. We would be pushing to get a conviction in any of the cases. And then there's the burden on the families. They have been waiting years to find out what happened to their loved ones and the plea agreement would give them the closure they so desperately need. Ma'am, I know it's up to you to decide, but in my opinion the plea deal is the only real option we have."

In the end, Sheila Brenton went for it. We heard about it the same way everyone else did—via a press conference on the county court steps. Surrounded by the victim's families, Sheila Brenton announced to the world that she was bringing Oregon's worst serial killer to justice and that the families would finally be reunited with their sisters and daughters. That same day Sheila Brenton announced she would be running for governor for a second term.

"Still there?" I say into the phone.

Novak exhales. "Yeah."

I hear his footsteps move through the undergrowth. The voices in the background fade to nothing.

"Jesus," he says.

I imagine him alone, resting against a tree trunk, washing his face with his hand.

"Have you slept?"

"Hawkins knows this means the plea deal is off, right?"

"O'Leary's arguing that Rex has acted in good faith and has been honest. He says Rex has a genuine intention to hold up his end of the deal, and is still willing to do so. They will fight us if we try and revoke the plea deal. This thing could be held up in court for years and we'll never be able to recover those women."

"How is this even happening?"

"He could be telling the truth. After all, he did give us some correct locations."

"Bullshit, he is," growls Novak. "Besides, what does it matter? He's got us over a barrel, either way. Son-of-a-bitch."

"Why don't you try talking with the governor. See if you can persuade her."

"Me? She won't listen to me. It needs to come from you, Amelia. You're the one who talked her into it last time."

I think of the ultrasound image of my baby. My baby with her tiny waving hand.

"Novak, I can't. I'm supposed to be taking it easy. Besides, you're the lead on the body recovery, she'll respect that."

"She's not going to listen to me. I'm telling you now."

"You don't know that."

There's a pause.

"We have history."

"What history?"

"I'd rather not get into that."

The penny drops. "You dated the governor?"

Eventually, Novak says, "We met at Columbia in our early twenties. We were freshmen. It ended badly. She hates me. Let's just leave it at that."

I think back to our meeting with the governor. That day Novak had pretty much left the talking up to me, but I never suspected they knew each other.

"You never said."

"I'm not exactly proud of it."

"Jesus, Novak." I take a breath. "Well, you're just going to have to suck it up and try. Apologize. Beg. Do whatever you have to and get her to agree. You don't have a choice because I'm not coming."

17

When I was nine, I found my father's dead body in our attic office. I'd been taking him up lunch—a peanut butter sandwich and a freshly baked oatmeal cookie I'd just made with my mom, all set out nicely on a tray with a gingham cloth. When I opened the door, the first thing I saw were his feet swaying in the air. To begin with, I just stood there, confused. Then I thought it must be a trick and I laughed. Sometimes my father did that. Trick me. Once he clutched his chest and pretended to be shot when a firecracker went off. Another time, he jumped out from behind a door to give me a fright.

I stopped laughing when I saw the taut nylon strap attached to the rafter. I remember my eyes drifting downward to the circumference of his neck, where the strap disappeared into the folds of his flesh. I had seen the neon-green strap before. We had used it once for towing my mother's car. At the time Mom had questioned whether it would be strong to take the weight of a vehicle, and my father, an engineer, had assured her that even though it was slim, the strap was strong enough to tow not only one car, but two.

I stood there too long, looking. I know I did. Thinking back, I often wonder if I'd gone and got help more quickly whether he might have survived.

Years later, when I was in therapy with Lorna after the incident with Rex, we talked about responsibility. I think she was trying to make me see that the suicide of my father was not the responsibility of my nine-year-old self. But what if those five minutes had made all the difference? What if I had gone and got help right away? They'd said he'd been dead for hours and there was nothing I could have done. But in my dreams, I'm pretty sure I remember him twitching.

I add the last sprinkle of cheese to the lasagna and slide it in the oven. For some reason, I'm thinking about all this now. There's a discomfort inside me that I don't like and I can't work out what it is. Like a piece of grit in my eye or stone in my shoe.

I turn on the timer for forty-five minutes and start tidying the mess in the kitchen. I rinse the empty tomato tins and put them in the recycling bin. I wrap the cheese and return it to the fridge. I scrub the stuck-on ground beef from the saucepan and place it the cupboard beneath the counter. Still, the ghostly image of my father's swinging feet won't leave me.

I sit down at the table and put my head in my hands. Not this, not this on top of everything else.

I check my phone. Nothing from Novak. Did I just blow that entire thing, too? Then I hear Lorna's soft voice intone, "Not everything is your responsibility to fix, Amelia. There are some things outside of your control."

I hear the key turn in the lock and Ethan enters.

"Hey, beautiful," he says, face lighting up when he sees me. He glances at the oven all aglow and emitting lovely aromas. "No way—is that lasagna?"

I give him a smile. "Specially for you."

"For me?"

"Husband number two's turn tomorrow night."

"Oh yeah, and what's his gig?" he says, hanging his coat on the hook next to the door.

99

"Baked chicken and mashed potatoes."

Ethan kisses the top of my head. "Funny girl." He sits down next to me. "How was your day?"

I don't say anything about the mess with Rex. I'm not sure why.

I look at him. "I'm sorry," I say. "About last night. About the fight."

"Fight? What fight?" He smiles, teasing me. "Oh, you mean our heated parenting discussion."

"I'm being serious, Ethan." I put my hand in my pocket and feel the corners of the ultrasound image. "I could have handled things better."

He nods, looks serious. "Me, too."

My phone rings. It's Novak. "Sorry, I better take this."

Ethan winks at me and gets up. "I need a shower anyway."

I wait until he's out of the room before answering.

"Novak? What's happening?" I say in a low voice.

"Brenton won't go for it," he sighs. "She says the plea deal is off, too."

I feel the pulse thump at the base of my throat. "She can't do that."

"She just did."

"What did you say to her?"

"Whoa. This isn't my fault, Amelia."

"Novak, you have to go back. You need to try harder."

"I told you already. She hates me." He pauses. "You gotta come here, Amelia. You can get her to change her mind. She respects you. You need to do it before she makes some sort of public announcement because she'll never back down after that."

"Novak, I can't. The baby, and I promised Ethan I would take it easy after the interview."

"The families have been calling. They want to know what's going on."

I exhale. "What a goddamn mess."

"Yeah," says Novak, letting out a breath, too. "It's a veritable shit show."

*

By the time Ethan finishes showering, I'm packing an overnight bag.

"What are you doing?" he says, halting in the doorway, towel wrapped around his waist.

"I'm sorry, Ethan. I don't have a choice."

"What do you mean you don't have a choice? What's going on? Is the baby all right?"

"She's fine. There's been a development about the search."

He walks over to me. "I'm listening."

"They can't locate some of the bodies. Rex says he needs to go to Oregon to see the scenes for himself but the governor won't allow it. I need to change her mind."

"You can't travel this far along. It's not safe."

"I rang Sandy Liu. She said, on balance, it would probably be okay."

"On balance? Probably?"

"You know doctors. They don't like to give black-and-white answers. They want to cover themselves."

He throws his hands up in the air. "Yeah, in case something goes wrong and you don't sue them for malpractice."

"Nothing's going to go wrong, Ethan. All I have to do is sit on a plane."

101

"Amelia, this is stupid. Let someone else do it. You need to take a step back. You promised me."

I glance at him and his disappointed face.

"This entire thing is about to fall apart. There isn't anybody else," I say.

"What if I ask you not to go?"

I stop folding my nightgown and look at him. "What do you mean?"

"Don't go," he says.

I remain silent.

"You have to stop trying to save the world at some point, Amelia."

I continue packing. "You knew this about me when you married me. I can't not go." My phone beeps. "The car is here." I zip up my bag and look at him. "I'll be back before you know it."

18

Novak and March are waiting for me in the darkened terminal of Salem Municipal Airport, a small non-commercial airport mainly used for light aircraft like the FBI Cessna I just arrived in. It's nearly 3 a.m. and the place is eerily empty. Cold too, I think as I shiver beneath my coat.

"I hope you guys haven't been waiting too long," I say.

Out of the two of them, Novak looks the worse for wear. While March is her usual put-together self, with her button-up white shirt, sensible trouser suit, and hair neatly tied back, Novak has not shaved for at least a week, and there's dirt all over his jeans and boots and a terrible look of exhaustion etched into his face. I take a guess and conclude there hasn't been much sleep for him over the last week and the issue with the governor can't have helped.

"Still gigantic, I see," says Novak, taking my overnight bag.

"And you've lost none of your charm."

He shoots me a weary smile. "I aim to please."

The three of us head toward the exit.

"Did you manage to sleep on the flight, Ms. Kellaway?" says March.

"Unfortunately not."

"The small planes can be noisy."

But it wasn't the Cessna's engine that had kept me awake. It was Ethan. The image of his crestfallen face as I had walked out the door. It'll be all right, I tell myself.

Once this is over, he'll realize everything was for the greater good, then we can get on with our lives.

We drive the two miles from the airport and cross the Marion Street bridge over the Willamette River into the dark streets of downtown Salem. Apart from a few sweeper trucks clearing trash from the gutters, the place is deserted at this time of morning.

Novak pulls up outside a Denny's and cuts the engine. "We got a few hours to kill before the governor arrives at her office. I need to eat, everyone okay with that?" he says.

March and I don't object, so we go inside and take a booth down the back. Novak orders a full breakfast, while March and I stick to coffee.

Novak removes a folder from his satchel and slides it across the table. "The security protocol you asked for."

I flip it open and take a look. I'm pleased. They've been very thorough. The protocol outlines that in addition to local law enforcement, a number of extra armed agents will be present, including two master snipers. The protocol also explains the precise routes the convoy will take to the sites, including any necessary road closures, and a recapture strategy should the worst happen and Rex was to escape. There was even a military helicopter with heat-seeking capability on standby.

"This all looks good," I say, closing the file. "What time is the meeting with Governor Brenton?"

Novak lowers his gaze. "Yeah, about that."

I don't like where this is going. "What is it?"

"She won't take my calls."

I feel my blood pressure rise and my monitor bleeps. "What do you mean, she won't take your calls? Do I have a scheduled meeting with her or don't I?"

104

"Not exactly."

"Not exactly or no, Novak?"

He pauses. "No."

I glance at March. It's clear she knows nothing about this, either.

"I thought we could wait in the lobby, catch her before she goes up," he says.

"That's your plan?"

He nods.

Our food arrives and we fall silent until the waitress leaves.

"She'll talk to you if she sees you're here," says Novak.

"You should have told me."

"Would that have changed your mind about coming?"

I exhale. "No. Probably not. I guess we'll just have to do our best. What about the other thing you were going to organize? Can I rely on that?"

He nods. "Absolutely. Everything is set up." He looks at his watch. "In fact, March, you'd better get going."

*

Novak and I wait in the lobby of the Oregon State Capitol building. It's just after 8 a.m. and the place is humming with government workers toting briefcases and sipping Starbucks as they make their way to their respective posts in the State Legislature. The governor's office is on the second floor, but Novak and I make the decision to wait on the ground floor. We don't want to risk alerting the governor's executive assistant, who is, according to Novak, more protective of the governor's time than a pit bull with a side of ham.

Just before 9 a.m., Governor Sheila Brenton enters the building. Petite with a strong angular face, she is more handsome than beautiful. Deep in conversation on her cell, she strides across the foyer, her mid-heeled pumps striking the marble floor with authority and purpose.

Novak gives me a self-conscious glance as if to say, yeah, I know, not my usual type, but I can understand the attraction. She's a woman who holds herself like she knows her own power, one who stands her ground and has probably worked extremely hard to get where she is today. That kind of confidence could be very appealing to men.

Wrestling with my cane, I rise from the lobby couch and call out to her before she disappears into the elevator alcove.

"Governor Brenton, may I have a word?"

She lifts her head at the sound of her name. She looks at my face, then her eyes drop to my cane. I see that hazy I-know-you-from-somewhere look cloud her face. Then she spots Novak and her lips tighten. I wonder if she suspects how much private hurt she is leaching out into the world.

She raises a finger at me to wait while she finishes her phone call.

When she's done, she looks at me. "How can I help?"

I extend my hand, which she takes.

"Amelia Kellaway," I say. "Assistant district attorney on the Hawkins case. We met during plea negotiations."

"I remember." Her voice has a clipped weighty tone to it. She looks at Novak. "I don't appreciate the ambush."

Novak is wise enough to keep quiet.

"I know. I'm sorry," I say. "My trip was short notice. Perhaps we could talk in your office?"

"You won't change my mind."

"I just want to talk."

106

She gives me a direct look. "I'm not in the habit of going around in circles, Ms. Kellaway. It's unproductive, not to mention a waste of everybody's precious time. I made my position very clear to Special Agent Novak yesterday, which he has no doubt explained to you. No field trips. No plea deal."

"If you'll just hear me out."

"I don't wish to relitigate this. I've made my decision. Now if you'll excuse me."

She turns and heads for the lift. I hurry after her in my indelicate waddling, cane-clapping way.

"Please, Governor, I just need five minutes." I clutch her arm. She stops and looks down at my hand. "I need to know I have done everything I can for the families."

I hear the vulnerability in my voice and hope she can hear it too. She looks thoughtful. Her eyes run the length of my cane, stopping at my foot and ugly orthopedic shoe.

"He hurt you, too, didn't he?"

"Yes."

Sheila Brenton pauses, considering.

"Very well. You'd better come up."

19

Governor Brenton gestures to the pretty brocaded chair. "Please, take a seat."

I lower myself into the chair and look around the room. Stately with wood-paneled walls, the governor's office is both officious and elegant. To the left there's a beautiful glass-fronted walnut cabinet housing an array of items, including a marble bust of Lincoln and a gilded pine cone in a Plexiglas display case. An impressive hand-drawn map of the State of Oregon hangs above the fireplace, and to the right, a cluster of framed photographs of handshakes with dignitaries is displayed on the wall. On the floor next to the governor's desk, I spy a box of campaign flyers and a large container of "Vote for Brenton" lapel buttons. Clear reminders there's an election in full swing and I need to tread carefully.

The governor sits in the gray leather director's chair behind her desk, and laces her fingers together. "I'm listening," she says.

I glance at Novak, who's leaning against the window frame keeping quiet. He gives me a barely perceptible nod.

I take a breath. "Governor Brenton," I say, "I don't know if Rex Hawkins is telling us the truth, I really don't, but what I do know is that the families want their sisters and daughters back home and there is simply no other way. They have been through so much already and they need closure to be able to move on with their lives. Not only that—we need to think of the victims, too. They deserve to be treated with respect and dignity, even in death. They deserve a proper funeral, and whether we like it or not, without Rex Hawkins they will not get one." I pull out the security protocol and slide it across her desk. "The security plan would allow Rex Hawkins forty-eight hours, and forty-eight hours only. Under a heavily armed contingent, there would be little to no risk of escape. If there's so much as a foot in the wrong direction, armed snipers will take him out, and if, after the forty-eight hours is up, Hawkins fails to deliver, then we throw out the plea deal and the death penalty is back on the table."

The governor pauses. "It's not just a safety issue, Ms. Kellaway. There are broader factors at play here, ones that affect the entire community. For instance, the region relies heavily on tourism. Local industry has worked very hard to promote a clean, green, family-friendly state and is just getting back on its feet. What do you think this serial-killer-dumping-ground debacle is doing for that? The entire thing has already been very damaging to the local economy, and letting Hawkins come here will only perpetuate the three-ring circus and make matters worse."

I keep my eye contact strong and say, "With respect, Governor, people will forget."

Sheila Brenton gives me a doubtful look. "And in the meantime, who suffers? I'll tell you who—decent, local families who rely on tourism for employment, that's who. And for what? So some twisted killer gets a field trip? Besides that, I've been elected on a law and order platform. My mandate from the people is be tough on crime and they rely on me to deliver that. Not to mention the fact that the community needs consistency from their elected leaders."

"Sheila, be reasonable," says Novak.

She looks at him. "And what if Hawkins does escape?" she says. "Can you imagine the fall-out from that? Even though I accept the risk is low, there is still a risk. He could take a hostage, kill someone, anything. It would be a catastrophe. And who do you think they would blame?"

Novak groans. "Sheila, that's not going to happen. Hawkins won't be able to cough without someone putting a bullet between his eyes."

She shakes her head, adamant. "You cannot guarantee that, Steve. You simply cannot. No, I'm sorry. You've given me nothing new here to change my mind. The risk, on multiple levels, is simply too great. You'll have to think of some other way."

"You're just concerned for yourself," growls Novak.

I freeze. "Novak, please."

The governor's lips tighten. "I'm sorry? What did you say to me?"

"Don't kid yourself, Sheila. This isn't about the community, it's about you and the election."

Novak pushes himself off the wall and approaches her and I feel my heart sink.

"Novak, please let me handle this," I implore.

He ignores me and points a finger at Sheila Brenton. "It's about you pandering to business leaders. It's about you not wanting to risk campaign dollars. It's about you wanting to keep your goddamn job."

Sheila rises from her seat. "How dare you."

"Tell me it isn't true," challenges Novak.

"Get out," she says, pointing to the door.

Novak looks at her for a second, shaking his head. "What happened to you, Sheila? I used to admire you so much for standing up for what's right."

He leaves, slamming the door behind him. I sit there awkwardly, not sure what to do.

"I'm sorry," I say. "It's been a tough week for him."

The governor turns her back and looks out the window as she tries to collect herself.

"This job isn't easy, Ms. Kellaway," she says. "Balancing these competing interests. Thinking about the greater good." She turns to me. "I've done a lot of good for the community, and I can do more. I want to continue to serve. I have great sympathy for the families, but the risk is simply too great."

I feel the weight of disappointment wash over me. "Governor, please."

"I'm sorry, but my answer is no."

There's a knock on the door. Julie, the governor's executive assistant, steps into the room looking a little pale.

"What is it, Julie?"

"Some of the victims' families are here, ma'am. They're waiting outside."

"What do you mean?"

"They've brought reporters."

Governor Brenton looks at me. "Are you responsible for this?"

"They just want to talk," I say.

"Unbelievable," she says, flinging up her hands.

"Just hear them out."

"This is totally inappropriate."

"They're desperate, Governor. Please understand."

She throws back her head and blinks at the ceiling. "God."

"What would you like me to do, ma'am?" says Julie.

The governor lets out a breath. "Send them in."

*

An hour later, as Novak, March, and I wait in a nearby coffee shop, we get the call.

Sheila Brenton's steely voice fills the line. "You've got forty-eight hours."

20

"Have you ever thought about escaping, Rex?" Stan whispers into the dark.

"You getting sick of me, Stan?"

The springs of the top bunk creak as Stan leans over the side. The boy's ready for a big discussion but Rex just wants to sleep.

"Course not, Rex. Sometimes I just wonder about it, that's all—what it would be like to get out of here. It's been such a long time since I've seen the outside." He pauses. "It's a fact that I'm going to die in here."

Rex keeps his eyes closed, not wanting to show any sign of encouragement. "People die out there, too, Stan."

"But how would you do it, if you were going to?"

Rex rolls over and pulls the prickly blanket over his shoulders. "Best you get these notions out of your head, Stan. That kind of thinking will drive you crazy."

Stan falls quiet and Rex begins to drift off. It had been a long day. He wants to be fresh for the morning.

"Before you came, a few years ago, someone tried," says Stan. "A Mexican dude. He scaled the fence during rec time and they shot him right there on the spot. I think he was high. I saw a documentary once about this one guy in France, a bank robber. His wife rented a helicopter and landed it on the prison roof to pick him up. They got away, too. He got killed in a shootout later though." Stan pauses. "You'd need help on the outside, I guess, to make it work. I got no one like that. If you do escape, Rex, can I have the ship-in-the-bottle?"

"Go to sleep, Stan."

"What time are they coming for you?"

"Early."

"You might be on the news."

Rex stays quiet and Stan lies back down.

"Just saying, I'll miss you, that's all. If you did escape." Then, a few seconds later, "Are you going in an airplane?"

"I expect that to be the case, Stan."

"I've never been in an airplane. I've never even been out of state. You think it will be a private jet or one of those commercial liners so you'll be sitting there with everyone else?"

Rex sighs. "Stan."

"Sorry, Rex. I'll shut my trap and let you get some sleep."

He falls silent. Outside the cell, the pipes creak and someone moans. Or cries. It's hard to tell in here.

"One last thing, Rex?"

Rex exhales. "What is it, Stan?"

"Wake me up before you go so I can say goodbye."

*

Bruce comes for Rex at four in the morning. Stan's fast asleep with his eyes wide open. Which isn't unusual for him. The boy has done it for the entire time Rex has known him. It is one of the strangest quirks in a human being that Rex has ever encountered. When Rex first noticed Stan doing it, he thought the boy was dead and he got a hell of a fright when Stan woke up and began talking as normal. Rex later found out it was actually a thing—nocturnal lagophthalmos, or something similar.

Rex takes nothing, just his canvas shoes, which he puts on outside the cell so he won't wake Stan. Bruce escorts him out of C Wing, stopping once they are buzzed into the corridor to put on Rex's belly and foot chains.

"Sorry about this, Rex, but they insisted," says Bruce, kneeling down to secure the fastening around Rex's ankles.

"Think nothing of it, Bruce. You're just doing your job."

They continue up the corridor, slower now because of the chains. Rex has never been out of the wing at this time of morning and the place has a deserted feel, like an abandoned hospital or underground bunker. They pass through a warren of hallways and a number of secure doors until they reach an exit unfamiliar to Rex. A blast of cold air hits them when Bruce opens the door into what looks to be a vehicle bay where deliveries are made.

Standing at the bottom of the concrete slope are two men in suits. Four more men dressed head to toe in full SWAT gear are positioned on the outer rim, semi-automatics pointed at Rex.

"What a side show," mutters Bruce.

"They just want to be sure I'm not going to do anything stupid."

One of the men walks up the ramp. "That'll be all," he says.

Bruce hesitates.

"I'm fine, Bruce. I'll see you in a bit," says Rex.

Bruce nods. "Best of luck, Rex."

Bruce disappears through the doorway and Rex is left alone with the welcoming committee. He glances around at the men in SWAT gear while one of the suited men, who Rex guesses is FBI, checks that Rex's chains are secure. In a way, it is a shame, the mistrust. Still, people are afraid of what they don't understand and there is no use in appointing blame or getting your nose out of joint.

Rex wonders what he would have to do for one of them to shoot him. He wonders whether they would go for the head or the heart first. And if the worst did happen and he was to lose his life, he wonders if the man who fired the fatal shot would be able to live with himself. Probably, Rex concludes. They are trained soldiers, after all. Professionals. Able to sort the wheat from the chaff. Not that different from him.

Satisfied the chains are okay, the FBI agent takes Rex by the arm and leads him to an idling SUV parked at an angle a few feet away. As the agent reaches across to buckle Rex into the seat, his suit jacket flaps open. Rex's eyes drop to the handgun nested in the black leather holster. An FBI-issued Glock 17 9mm. A lightweight, reliable auto-loader with a seventeen-round magazine. It's a careless mistake. So easy to reach for. In two simple moves Rex could snatch it and shoot the man in the head.

"You got a name, son?" Rex says instead.

The man looks at him, his blue eyes contemplating.

"Blake."

"I won't cause you any trouble, Blake, you can be sure of that."

The man gives Rex a nod and then takes a seat in the front with his partner. He punches a number into his phone and speaks. "ETA to the airfield, fifteen minutes."

*

Later, on lift-off, Rex thinks about how he just saved Blake's life. Then he leans back and closes his eyes and sleeps like a baby.

21

As the first rays of dawn rise above the pines, I wait on the back road to Highway 97 with Novak and March. At any other time, this road would be quiet but right now it's a hive of activity. Like something out of *The Fugitive*. Flashing patrol lights. Armed officers. Steel barriers.

Governor Brenton had insisted we involve local law enforcement, so in addition to the FBI SWAT team there are county police from Medford here, too. A dozen or so stand near their patrol cars with rifles looking slightly bewildered. In contrast, the FBI contingent are well organized and have taken up strategic positions along the road, ready to pop a bullet into Rex's skull at a split second's notice.

It has just begun to rain lightly. A patter against the asphalt and on top of the car. I look up and say a silent prayer for the weather to hold. The next forty-eight hours will be critical—if we don't get this thing done now, it will never happen.

I pull on my hood and suck in an icy breath. The dank fresh smell of the forest fills my lungs. It feels good, lively. I think of Bernetta James. A mile inland from here, up an old dirt road near a trail close to Crater Lake National Park, was where her last resting place was supposed to have been. Through the wall of pines, it's possible to just make out the blurred halo of the floodlight erected during the earlier failed search attempt.

Once Rex arrives, we will go in there and try again. Next time there will be no failure. Next time we will return with Bernetta James's body. I will make sure of it.

My phone buzzes in my pocket. I take a look. It's a message from Ethan. Good luck for today. I feel a deep regret as I slide the phone back into my pocket. There had been another heated discussion on the phone last night. He accused me of misleading him.

"You said you would be right back after speaking with the governor."

"Ethan, it's only another forty-eight hours and I need to be here if something comes up."

"You're going to do what you're going do no matter what I say or think."

"That's not true. I care about what you think."

"Well, you could've fooled me."

Then he hung up on me. He had never done that before. Just hung up without saying goodbye. I feel the sting of it now and try to push it away.

There's a commotion up ahead and the FBI snipers shoulder their rifles. A trio of vehicles appear, one after the other.

"Looks like we got company," utters Novak.

I keep my eyes fixed on the road, conscious of my tightening chest. The first vehicle stops near us and a tall, youthful-looking agent gets out and opens the back door. A few seconds later, Rex exits. He stands there, looking at the forest. He throws his head back and blinks at the drizzly, gray sky, a smile on his lips.

"Hello, Rex," I say.

Rex lowers his head, frowning when he sees me. "Amelia? Should you be here in your condition?"

118

"Why don't you let me worry about that."

"I know what you must be thinking," he says, "that I'm working some sort of angle. But that really isn't so. My memory isn't what it used to be, that's all. I'm sure being here will make things clearer."

"We just want to find the women, Rex."

He nods. "I know you do and we will."

Novak shakes the agent's hand. "Hello, Blake. Good to see you. March and Amelia, this is Special Agent Blake Jenkins. He's the security detail who'll be joining us."

I notice March color slightly. I don't blame her. Blake is a good-looking guy, no wedding ring either.

Novak says, "March, you and Blake will be in the back with Hawkins. He tries anything, you got my permission to blow his head off."

"I'm not looking to cause any trouble," says Rex.

Novak glares at him for a second then continues. "The plan is we go into the search site, get him to take a look around, see what he remembers. Once we get out of the car, everyone moves real slow. There's a lot of happy trigger fingers here and I don't want any accidents. Everyone clear on that?"

We nod.

"Good," says Novak, satisfied. "Let's get this show on the road."

22

We journey inland to the failed search site, taking the long, twisting dirt road deep into the forest. Novak does his best to navigate the uneven surface, but the unsealed road is rough, causing us to jerk back and forth in our seats. I feel a little sick, but I'm okay. I took a nausea tablet earlier which has helped, and damned if I'm going to show any sign of weakness in front of Rex.

Everyone is quiet. Me and Novak in the front, March, Blake, and Rex in the back. The only sounds are from the stones sporadically pinging along the car's undercarriage and the windshield wipers whirring back and forth in a frenzy. The rain has gotten bad, way worse than I had feared. Still, our destination should be protected by the canopy of the trees so I'm hoping we'll be spared the worst.

Novak carries on over a rise and the floodlight grows more prominent through the trees, like the eerie glow of a spaceship that has landed in the middle of nowhere. We reach the site and Novak pulls up next to a mustard-colored mini-digger parked an angle, its steel, claw-like arm frozen in mid-air. To the right of that, tape sections off a large area with mounds of dirt, reminders of the earlier fruitless attempts to find Bernetta's body.

Rex stares out the window. "It all looks so different now."

Novak glances over his shoulder at him. "I don't want to hear any fucking excuses, Hawkins, just show us where she is."

Bernetta James, thirty-two. A nurse at a local community hospital in Bend, Oregon. According to her ailing mother, in 1987 Bernetta was just getting her life together after a bitter divorce in which her church-going husband was found to be having intimate relations with a much younger parishioner. The marriage had produced no children—"Thank God for that," said her mother—but had caused a lot of heartache and self-doubt. Which was why Bernetta James had decided to take up trekking on the weekends—to help build up her confidence and detangle the emotional remnants of the divorce.

Bernetta took a real liking to the solo pursuit, and nearly every weekend would pack up her car and explore one of the trails in the national parks. Her mother once asked Bernetta why she liked it so much and Bernetta had simply replied, "It clears my head."

In fact, her mother said that Bernetta was getting so confident in her abilities to take care of herself in the wilderness, she was thinking of going to the Pacific Crest trail that summer. She never made it. Any future she might have had vanished the weekend she decided to do a day trek around Crater Rim Lake and encountered the stranger in the pale green Ford Capri.

According to Rex's interview, he first saw Bernetta at the parking lot at the bottom of the trail. They chatted for a bit and she told him she was just about to embark on a day hike. As she was about to leave, Rex helpfully identified that the front tire of Bernetta's VW was looking a little flat and offered to take a look.

After that things happened quickly. Rex knew Crater Rim Lake was a popular spot and it was likely other visitors would soon been arriving so he wasted no time in knocking Bernetta James out, striking her with a fist full to the face before bundling her limp and compliant body into the trunk of his car. He took her deep into the woods and kept her alive for two nights. But as the new work week approached, Rex had the good sense to know that people would start looking for Bernetta. She was not a lone traveler or out of town visitor; this was a local woman with family and friends.

According to Rex, Bernetta James took approximately seven minutes to die. The date of her death was May 28, 1987. After he strangled her, he dumped her body in a dirt grave and fled.

I glance down at the hole where Bernetta James was supposed to have been. It's beginning to fill with mud. Rex looks at it, too.

"No, this isn't right," he says, frowning.

He lifts his head and looks around. I wonder what he sees. It all looks the same to me. Woods and more woods.

"Can we go further in?" he says.

"How far?" says Novak.

Rex looks at him. "We should drive."

23

As I see-saw in my seat, I'm not convinced that Rex isn't leading us on a wild goose chase. But we're at his mercy, whether we like it or not. I can tell that Novak feels the same. The tautness in his neck betrays him. The tight white knuckles gripping the steering wheel. The look of resentment playing across his face.

I reach forward and angle the vents of the heater toward me. The deeper in we go the colder it gets. The rain is barely visible here, though, because the forest is so thick. Thick and dark and isolated. My eyes flick to the wing mirror. Behind us, two FBI SUVs follow closely. I'm not sure it brings me any comfort. If Rex has a plan, if he really wanted to kill us or escape, he would.

His eyes have been glued to the window this whole time. He appears to be searching. Every once in a while, he mutters something under his breath but I can't quite catch what it is.

The tracks we are following appear to belong to an old logging trail. The occasional tree, felled long ago, lies across the forest floor, moss covered and darkening with decay. I spy a set of rusty chains. Nearby there's a pulley and a few feet of steel tracks that disappear into nothing.

Novak looks in the rearview. "Anything?"

"Keep going," he says.

Novak gives me a look and we travel on, lurching in our seats as the terrain grows even rockier.

"Stop here."

Novak halts the car.

"Yes, yes," says Rex, looking out the window. "This is it."

We get out. A small contingent made up of an FBI sniper, two members of the SWAT team, and two special agents form a half circle around us. They keep pace as Rex leads us into the thickest part of the woods. Even with everyone here, the place seems lonesome and foreboding. Like we are survivors of a plane wreck lost in the woods. We move forward, merging with the dim shadows of the pines. I look over my shoulder. The vehicles seem very far away. I begin to sweat beneath my coat.

A stick cracks underfoot and I'm catapulted back in time, when I am running for my life, when Rex is chasing me. A wave of nausea rises up my throat and I have to stop.

March touches my arm. "Ms. Kellaway?"

I'm about to tell her I'm fine when I vomit violently into a pile of pine needles. In the background, I hear Rex ask if I'm all right. I heave again, caught between extreme embarrassment and searing anger. At myself. At him. I do not want him to see me like this.

"I'm fine. I'm fine," I say, straightening up.

The baby somersaults and presses down on my pelvis and I double over again.

"Give her a minute," March calls to the others.

I look at them through watering eyes and plaster a calm look on my face.

"Everyone, I'm okay. Really. Please carry on without me and I'll catch up."

I'm surprised at how reasonable I sound. I wait until they start moving then let out a breath. March steers me to a rock so I can sit down.

"Thank you, March. You're very kind."

We stay there for a time, me sitting, March standing.

"I can't imagine what it would have been like for you," she says, finally.

My eyes sweep across the forest. "Just when I think it's behind me, there'll be some sort of a trigger."

"It must be very hard."

I nod. "It is but at least I'm alive. The others weren't so lucky."

"Yes," says March. "That's not nothing. And look what you're doing now, helping bring all those other women home."

"It's ironic."

She looks at me, blinking. "That's not irony, Ms. Kellaway, that's God."

We rejoin the group. Rex glances over his shoulder and gives me a look of concern. I ignore it and we continue on, walking through the undergrowth, weaving through the trees.

Novak is getting frustrated. "This is a total waste of time," he growls.

Rex stops and looks around.

"What is it?" I say. "Do you recognize something?"

"Yes," he says. "Yes, I think I do." His eyes land on a ridge a few feet ahead. "Up there, in fact."

"You better not be bullshitting us," says Novak.

Rex shakes his head. "I've seen it before. I remember."

How Rex could possibly recognize the area is beyond me. As far as I can tell, there are no landmarks or anything else to differentiate it from the rest of the woods. But Rex seems sure so we follow him.

Even though the incline is modest, I have trouble keeping up. My heart batters in my chest and I begin to feel sick again. March, bless her, sticks close. And, once or twice, I reach out to steady myself against her arm. When we crest the ridge, Rex stops.

He frowns and shakes his head. "I'm sorry."

I follow his gaze. More forest. More of the same.

He looks bereft. "I was wrong. This isn't it. I must be confused. I want to help. I really do."

"For fuck's sake," spits Novak. "Do you have any fucking idea where Bernetta James is?"

Rex's shoulders sag. "I can't be sure."

Novak grabs Rex by the shirt. "You'd better get sure then, hadn't you, Hawkins?"

I step forward. "Why don't we take a break? Consider our options."

"I would appreciate that, Amelia," says Rex. "Maybe something will come to me if I have some time to think."

We rest for a good ten minutes. Blake and Rex sit side-by-side, handcuffed at the wrists, on the highest point of the ridge while the security contingent position themselves at a discreet distance. Novak and I take a seat on a fallen log further down. Novak smokes aggressively. I wonder when he last got some sleep.

"This fucking guy…" he says.

I dig in my pocket for a mint—there's a foul taste in my mouth and the cigarette smoke isn't exactly helping—but my pocket's empty apart from a crumpled Kleenex and an ancient subway ticket.

"You think he's stalling?" asks Novak.

"Honestly, I don't know."

Novak blows smoke downwind. "Maybe we should turn back, try for the other two bodies. Otherwise we are going

126

to run out of time. We've only got him for forty-eight hours."

I think of Bernetta's elderly mother. The little shrine of her dead daughter on the mantel above the unused fireplace.

"Give him some time," I say. "Something might come to him."

Novak looks at me. "What happened back there?"

I lower my eyes. "It was nothing."

He glances around, taking in the trees. "It can't be easy. Coming here, with him."

"No."

"I read about you, you know. Before we met."

I wasn't surprised. I was used to everyone knowing about me—the lone woman traveler who survived being kidnapped, raped, and nearly murdered. I knew that depending on their point of view, their perceptions of me ranged from naive to stupid to courageous to determined.

"How long did he hold you captive for?"

"Four days."

"Then you escaped?"

"He thought he'd killed me and left me for dead, so technically no, I didn't escape."

"But you got away?"

I nod. "I had another three weeks in the woods on my own before I got out."

Novak whistles through his teeth. "Amazing. You must have been one determined lady."

"It seems like it happened to someone else now."

He glances at my belly. "Will you ever tell your daughter?"

I put a hand on my belly. "When she's old enough, yes."

"And your foot?'

I smile at his nerve. "Not many people are brave enough to ask me about that."

He stamps out his cigarette. "Sorry. I need to learn to shut my mouth."

"It got infected. I nearly died, actually."

"I nearly died, actually..." he says, teasing me. "You're quite something, aren't you, Amelia Kellaway?"

I get to my feet. The last thing I need is Novak coming on to me. It's the last thing he needs, too. Up on the ridge there's movement. Blake and Rex approach us. Rex is smiling.

"I remember now. There was a reservoir."

24

At first, everyone's mystified. According to the map, no such reservoir exists. Then March uses her mobile to access her digital archives and discovers a previous map from early last century. And there it was. A small spring-fed reservoir. Developed and used by a logging company in the 1920s. Operational until 1975.

The reservoir is three miles to the east so we take the vehicles and circle back the way we came from. It's beyond frustrating. We are five hours into our precious forty-eight and have yet to locate any of the bodies.

Thankfully with the map's help, the reservoir isn't difficult to find. Novak's the first to spot it and pulls in close and we get out to examine the area. What had once been fed by underground springs now lies barren and overgrown with brush. The only sign of a man-made component is a small dam, comprised of cement blocks. Nature has reclaimed the rest.

It's raining hard and despite the hood on my jacket, I feel the rain dribble down my neck and soak into the back of my shirt. I crave the warmth of the car but wait with Rex and the others as he stands there looking.

I try and imagine the day he took Bernetta James. It had been the height of summer. Hot and dry. I think of the cool, clear waters of the reservoir glistening in the sun.

"I washed myself afterward," he says.

"After you buried her?" I say.

"Yes, that's correct, Amelia, after I buried her."

His eyes drift across the reservoir. He raises his arm and points to an old chain-link fence.

"Over there," he says.

"You sure?" says Novak.

Rex nods decisively. "I'm certain."

We walk the circumference, the rain beating down us, trying not to lose our footing on the slippery earth bordering the reservoir. We pause when we reach the rusty chain-link fence. Rex walks on a few feet until he's under the trees. He clutches the remnants of an old fence line and kneels down.

He brushes his hand over the surface of the ground and looks up at us. "Here," he says.

*

Sheltered by a canvas lean-to, Blake, Rex, March, and I watch as Novak and the two forensic technicians use small trowels to excavate the site a little at a time. March had the foresight to bring supplies, three boxes of high-protein nut bars and a flask of strong, black coffee, and we sit there sipping the steaming bitter liquid in plastic cups. I can't face the thought of food though, so the little foil packet lies unopened in front of me.

It's four in the afternoon and already getting dark. Novak and the technicians will soon need light. I pray they find something soon. We need to make progress.

Suddenly there's a commotion. Novak yells stop and holds up his hand.

"Looks like they got a hit," says Blake, standing.

Novak and the two technicians look down at the disturbed earth.

I lower my coffee and get to my feet. "Blake, you stay here with Rex. Laura, come with me."

We go over for a closer look. I stare into the hole. Looking back at me is the butterfly-shaped bone of a pelvis.

"Is she all there?" I say.

"We won't know for sure until we dig deeper," he says, grimly. Novak puts his hand on his hips and looks around the forest. "But, Amelia, thirty-plus years have passed, and what with the grave being so shallow, there's a possibility we won't be able to recover every last piece of her."

Poor Bernetta. Poor Bernetta's mother. Novak touches my shoulder.

"You're freezing. Go wait in the car. I can't have that husband of yours blaming me for you and your offspring's untimely demise due to pneumonia."

"I'm fine," I say. "Keep going."

I tear myself from that heart-wrenching sight and return to wait with the others.

An hour later, they are done and all that is left of Bernetta James is laid out on a bright blue tarp next to the grave. A full skeleton, thank God, including a small, ghostly, hollow-eyed skull. Some remnants of clothing, mainly fragments of a pair of khaki shorts and a yellow T-shirt. A pair of relatively intact thick-soled hiking boots. And a vibrant pink nylon day pack, the contents of which included a water bottle, a disintegrated granola bar, a paperback copy of *The Valley of the Dolls*, and a Pepsi-Cola bottle opener key fob with a set of house keys on it. The items are a pitiful sight. A stark reminder of how an innocent walk in the woods had turned into a woman's worst nightmare.

Novak joins us under the shelter. He's soaked to the skin and covered in dirt. March passes him a bottle of water and he chugs it back in one go.

When he's done, he wipes his mouth with the back of his hand and stares at Rex. "I hope you're happy with yourself."

Rex frowns. "Of course I'm not happy."

"Don't give me that bullshit, Hawkins. You're lapping this up. All your handiwork on display for everyone to see."

"That isn't true," protests Rex.

But it's there. The slight pride in his voice. We all hear it.

Novak bares his teeth. "Blake, get this sick fuck out of here before I do something I regret."

25

It's after six by the time Bernetta's body is removed from the site. It's dark and cold and wet. Miserable conditions for everyone. The team is dispersed around the place, the FBI conversing in their SUV while the SWAT team remain at their posts, eyes trained on Rex, Blake, March, and I as we wait in the lean-to. Novak sees off the body removal van then joins us, somber-faced and tired.

He looks at his watch. "The other site's an hour's east of here, near the Fremont-Winema National Forest. Caitlyn McLellan, the twenty-two-year-old. We should get going." He shoots Rex a hard look. "Any complaints about that, Hawkins?"

Rex shakes his head. "I'm ready to work through the night if I have to."

"Well, aren't you just the hero," mutters Novak.

Rex looks put out. "I gave you Bernetta, didn't I? Just like I said I would."

"What you gave us, Hawkins, was the run-around and I don't want that happening again, do you understand me?"

Rex holds his gaze. "Whatever you say, Special Agent Novak."

Things are getting tense and I'm grateful to see one of the FBI agents lope toward us. Mike Chamberlain, a Boston native, who led the Sandy Hook body recovery.

"Bad news," he says, holding his cell phone to his chest. "There's flooding in Fremont Forest Park. Serious, apparently."

Novak's pissed. "You're shitting me."

Mike shakes his head. "I wish I was."

I look at the rain coming down outside the tent.

"Any idea when's its predicted to ease?"

"They're saying it could last for days, ma'am."

"Perfect," says Novak.

Mike tips his phone. "What do you want me to tell them? Postpone until daylight?"

Novak stands there, thinking.

"Look," he says. "I know it's a risk, but I say we go for it."

I stare at him. "You want to go to Fremont Park while it's flooded?"

He nods. "We just carry on up there and if the flooding's too bad when we get there, we pull back and stop for the night."

No one says anything.

"I agree," says March.

"Laura, are you sure?" I say.

"Yes, Ms. Kellaway. We might as well go and take a look. It might not be as bad as they say. It's the only way we're going to know for sure."

I turn to Blake and Mike. "And what about you two?"

"I say it's worth a shot," say Mike.

Blake nods. "Ditto that."

I stand there, thinking. "All right," I say, finally. "We go there and assess the situation. If there's a risk to life we don't go in. Understood, Novak?"

He nods. "You're the boss."

*

We continue on up the central divide, taking Route 97 for about an hour until we reach an intersection, then head west along a lonesome back road. The road's sealed but unlit, apart from the periodic flash of the amber reflective markers studded along the shoulder. The radio plays softly in the background, a soulful male rendition of "Amazing Grace," which only adds to the strangeness of the situation. I stare at the mesmerizing glow of the GPS fixed to the dash as I listen to the words. *I once was lost and now I'm found. 'Twas blind but now I see.* If anyone else notices the irony, they aren't saying.

I glance over my shoulder. Rex is dozing, head back on the seat, eyes shut. Blake isn't being complacent, though. He remains alert, hand hovering close to his holster. I return to the front and stare out the windshield at the black miserable night. I doubt Blake will need his gun. Rex isn't going anywhere. He wants to see this thing through. I'm not sure whether it's solely driven by his ego or a genuine need to put things right. Maybe it's a combination of the two. But what does it matter as long as we get the women back to their families?

Up ahead, a road sign illuminates in the headlights. *Sour Bend Falls.* Novak turns left and takes a narrow side road. Behind us the other vehicles follow, their headlights sweeping across the line of firs as they make the turn. We continue on for about half a mile, stopping when we come to an overflowing gully.

I peer out the window at the rushing water. "How deep do you think it is?"

"Difficult to say," says Novak.

Rex points to the window control. "May I?" he says to Blake.

Blake nods and Rex lowers the window and looks out.

"You should be okay if you cross over to the right by the stones. It's shallow there, you can tell by the angle of the trees along the banks."

Novak zips up his jacket and pulls on his hood. "I'm not asking for your advice, Hawkins."

He opens the door and gets out. I watch in my wing mirror as he approaches Mike, who is already walking the length of the bank. Novak grabs a tree branch and checks the depth of the water. They stand there for a moment, hands on their hips, deep in discussion, then head back toward their respective vehicles.

When Novak gets in the driver's seat, I say, "You and Mike have a plan?"

Novak puts the gear in reverse and looks over his shoulder as he backs the car away from the gully.

"We're going to try for it. Mike's going first to see if it's safe, then the crew's van, then us, the SWAT team to come behind."

"Are you sure that's wise?"

He nods. "It's a good plan, Amelia. You just have to trust me."

Novak parks off to the side, angling the car so the headlights illuminate the gully crossing where Rex suggested. We wait in silence, engine idling, as Mike attempts to make the crossing in the FBI vehicle. I hold my breath as he edges the SUV out a little at a time. But Rex was right, the gully is relatively shallow and Mike makes it to the other side without incident.

Next comes the van. At first everything seems okay as it inches out into the gully. Then, quite suddenly, the van's nose dips into the water and the back tires begin to spin frantically.

"Stay here," says Novak, getting out.

He goes around to the trunk, digs inside, shuts it with a thud. I see the beam of his flashlight tracing the ground as he heads left, away from the van. He carries on for about ten yards then stops. He sweeps the light back and forth over the bank then continues left into a thicket of brush and disappears from view. A few minutes later he strides back toward us, the hood of his parka obscuring his face.

"I found another way across," he says, opening the door. "We can't take a vehicle because of the trees, but we can walk." He looks at me and March. "I'll go ahead with Blake and Hawkins to the site. You guys can catch up when they've got the van free."

March looks concerned. "But, sir, that's a breach of the security protocol."

"Oh, I think Hawkins will behave himself, March. He knows I wouldn't hesitate to blow his fucking head off if I need to, don't you, Hawkins?"

Rex shrugs. "Like I've said all along, I'm here to help, not cause trouble."

Blake and Rex join Novak outside, and I watch the three of them walk away with a sinking feeling.

"I don't like this, March."

"Me neither, Ms. Kellaway. Would you like me to call Mike?"

I turn around to look at her. "You mean go over Novak's head?"

She nods. "It's an option. For everyone's safety."

I sit there, thinking.

"No," I say, exhaling. "Let's assume Novak knows what he's doing."

137

March and I wait a full twenty minutes as they extract the van from the gully by piling rocks and logs under each tire for traction. One of the SWAT team, Davis, I think, lets out a cheer when the van finally takes off and makes it to the other side.

I look at March, who's swapped to the driver's seat in Novak's absence. "That's us, Laura. You got this?"

She nods. "I do."

March takes her time angling the car into the gully. As we roll forward, I glance out the side window at the rushing water. My heart lobs in my throat. It looks so deep and wild. Strong enough to lift up the vehicle and sweep it downstream.

March inches out further and water pounds the sides of the car.

"This is the deepest part, Ms. Kellaway," says March. "Hang on."

The car rocks from side-to-side. I grab hold of the handle above the doorway to steady myself.

When we are three-quarters across, March says, "We should be good from here."

As long as there's not a flash flood, I think. But March is right and I'm relieved when we make it across in one piece. She brings the car to a complete stop on the bank and receives a round of applause from the others who've been watching our progress.

She turns to me. "You're sweating," she says, smiling. "Did you think I couldn't do it?"

I return her smile. "I never doubted you for a second, Laura."

Everyone returns to their vehicles and we carry on up the road to the original body site. But when we arrive, there's no sign of Novak, Blake, and Rex.

"They've gone on without us," I say to March, irritated. "See if you can reach Novak on his cell. I'll go and talk to Mike."

I button my coat to the throat, pull on the hood, and step outside. I'm halfway over to Mike when a shot rings out. Instinctively I duck and cover my head. Another shot follows. Members of the SWAT team run past me. The only thing I can think of is that Rex must have escaped.

"Stay there!" shouts Mike.

But I don't. I run, too, heading for the woods like everyone else. Thoughts of Novak and Blake rush through my head. I should never have let them go on with Rex alone. I try to keep up with the others, cupping my stomach as I go, but it's futile, I'm barely at a jog with my useless half-foot. Breathless, I pause by a tree. An intense cramp suddenly hits me. It feels like my insides are being squeezed in a vise. Sweat Jesus. I breathe through it and mercifully it passes.

I hear shouting.

"That way!"

"Target to the left!"

I look around in the darkness and try and make sense of what's happening. All around me, the woods are alive with thumping boots and cracking branches. Helmet lights bob up and down through the trees like giant fireflies.

I keep going and reach a clearing. The howling wind and rain smashes into me, nearly knocking me off my feet. I consider turning back when I see March in the distance crouched over someone on the ground. My heart falls to the pit of my stomach.

I fight my way toward her through the bitter rain. When I reach her, my hand flies to my mouth. Blake is dead, shot between the eyes. Novak and Rex have been shot, too, but both are still alive, writhing in pain on the ground. I don't understand. What is Rex doing here? If he's not the shooter, who is? I hear the crack of another shot in the woods.

I shout over the driving wind, "What the hell is going on, Laura! Who's doing the shooting?"

The shooting stops. I hold my breath waiting for more but there's nothing. Something catches my eye to the left. It's Mike emerging from the woods. A wave of relief washes over me—he's still alive.

He holds up his phone when he reaches us. "Recognize him?"

It's a photo of man's body, clearly dead, flashlight illuminating his lifeless face. March and I look at each other.

Finally, I nod. "That's Randy Miller. One of the victims' brother."

26

I first met Randy Miller a year ago when March and I had been deep in the investigation stage of the plea deal, trying to track down all of Rex's possible known victims. There had been a hotline set up, which had produced thousands of tips, most of which turned out to be nothing. But one, a note about a nineteen-year-old local woman named Karen Miller, caught my attention. Randy Miller, the woman's brother, had phoned it in.

When I dialed the number to return the call, the man who answered sounded drunk.

"Randy Miller?"

"Yeah."

"I'm calling about your sister."

"You got news about Karen?" he said, thickly.

"I'm just following up on your call."

There'd been a pause. "I don't like talking on the phone. You best come see me."

March and I took the hour-long drive to Redwood, a small town just outside of Bend. When we arrived, I was surprised to see the address was for a return veterans drop-in center. The center was located in an old weatherboard house with a pretty porch set against the boundary of a park. We were shown into the lounge area by a clerk, where a bunch of men were playing cards.

"Randy, you got people," said the clerk.

When the man with the mop of blond hair turned around, I immediately saw the reason for his slurred speech. Part of his jaw was missing.

I introduced myself. "I'm Amelia Kellaway, and this is Special Agent Laura March."

He stood up. "There's a place out the back where we can talk."

Randy showed us to a small room with sloping ceilings which looked like it doubled as a library. On the left side near a small window overlooking the backyard, two large bookcases overflowed with thick, doorstopper novels. Wilbur Smith. Stephen King. Tom Clancy. Stacks of well-thumbed magazines about motorsports, fishing, boating, and hunting filled the lower tiers. I suspected most of the reading material was donated and made a mental note that when it came time for me and Ethan to move, I would find a similar veterans drop-in center in my area and put my unwanted books to good use.

March and I took a seat on the old paisley sofa by the window while Randy Miller sat in the wooden chair opposite.

He glanced down at my cane. "Which foot?" he said.

"Right. Partial amputation. Lucky they could save what they did."

He grunted and nodded. I tried not to look at his twisted jaw, but its grotesqueness was compelling and I was fascinated with it the same way I was when I first saw my own foot after the operation.

"Unexploded ordinance. Ramadi," he said. "My jaw shattered into a million different pieces. But I can drink, chew, and talk so I'm grateful. That's more than some guys get." He wiped a smidge of saliva edging from the corner of his mouth with his thumb and continued. "So you want to talk about Karen?"

I nodded. "Tell us more about the circumstances of her disappearance."

He looked at me. "This fucker, Hawkins whatever, you think he could be responsible?"

I shrugged. "It's possible. We'll take the details you give us today and cross-check them, see if there's any connection."

He seemed to accept this and relaxed a little.

"Karen was my twin. Two peas in a pod as my mother used to stay. Karen was always bossing over me even though, strictly speaking, I was older by three minutes." He leaned forward and slipped his hand into his back pocket and pulled out his wallet. He took out a photo and looked at it sadly before handing it to me. It was of the two of them, about fourteen years old, at some sort of water park. They were shooting down a hydro slide with their arms in the air, laughing.

"You look happy."

He nodded. "We were. Back then. We had a falling out when I was twenty-two. It was my fault, our mom got cancer and I just couldn't deal with it so I joined the service, and Karen was left carrying the load. I was a weak, selfish cocksucker," he said bitterly. "When Karen would write me letters about Mom's condition, I would just throw them away. I began drinking a lot around that time, too. It was during my tours of Iraq. I drank to cope. We all did. Anyway, Karen calls me one night and tells me Mom died. She asked me to come home for the funeral but I said I couldn't, which was a lie, they would have let me go if I put in a request. After that, the letters stopped arriving. To tell you the truth, it was a relief." He looked up, swallowing. "I know how terrible that sounds, and it was."

I thought of my mother's own battle with cancer two years ago and how close she came to death. "It can be frightening when a parent gets sick like that," I said. "We all react differently."

"I was a coward," he said, self-hatred burning in his eyes. "I needed to grow the hell up. I let everyone down, especially Karen."

"When did you realize she was missing?" said March.

"When I came back home after I got injured. I'd just finished rehab at the VA's care unit in Virginia and wanted to reconnect with her. I traveled back home to Seattle because I thought she would still be living in Mom's old house but it was vacant. All Mom's and Karen's stuff was still there but the house was locked up and the yard was overgrown. I thought maybe she moved away so I tracked down her best friend, Chrissy. She told me that Karen went missing in May of 2006, right after Mom's death." He took a long deep breath. "They had tried to get hold of me but it got lost in the system. I was floored."

"What else did Chrissy say?"

"She said that Karen wasn't coping too well after Mom's death and spent a lot of time at bars. Biker bars, on the outskirts of town. She got in with some bad people. Met a guy who beat up her pretty bad." He swallowed and shook his head.

"What makes you think there's any connection to Rex Hawkins?"

He pulled out a crumpled piece of paper folded into quarters. He opened it to reveal a map. "The last time anyone saw her was right around here." He pointed to the

Grand Junction turnoff. "I heard on the news that Hawkins had dumped another woman in the same area."

"Was there a police report taken at the time?" said March.

He nodded. "Yeah. Chrissy reported her missing when she couldn't get hold of her. Karen was supposed to go to one of Chrissy's kids' birthday parties but never showed."

March made a note to check the report later.

"But that's not a lot to connect Rex Hawkins with Karen, Randy. Especially considering she'd fallen in with the wrong crowd," I said.

He looked at me and pauses.

"Someone saw her get into a car," he said. "A blue Ford Capri."

A chill ran up my spine. The blue Ford Capri was one of three cars Rex owned, a favorite by all accounts, and the one he used when he kidnapped me. We publicized it during our hotline campaign.

I kept my voice even. "We'll check the patrol officer's report, make a few inquiries, and see where we get to."

But every part of my being was telling me it was Rex.

After we left, I turned to March.

"What's your thinking, Laura?"

She looked at me with her sober blue eyes. "Sounds like Hawkins to me, Ms. Kellaway."

Two weeks later, March confirmed there was a high likelihood that Rex was responsible for Karen's disappearance. He'd been in the area at the time, and the witness was certain she saw Karen get into a blue Ford Capri. Then, finally, we heard it straight from the horse's mouth when, during the early days of drafting the plea deal, Rex confirmed he had kidnapped and murdered Karen.

I still remember the day I phoned Randy to tell him. For a long while he had said nothing, then thanked me and hung up the phone. The last time I saw him was on the news five days ago. He'd been watching from behind a cordon in the woods as they loaded Karen's body into a black hearse to take her to a mortuary.

Now it's his turn.

I pull my jacket tight around my shoulders and watch as Mike and the others emerge from the woods carrying Randy Miller in a body bag.

Someone touches my shoulder. It's March. "We should get to the hospital, Ms. Kellaway. Novak and Hawkins will be there by now."

I glance at the woods. I think of Caitlyn McLellan still out here somewhere.

"There's nothing more we can do here," says March.

The wind rises hard and strong. I watch the leaves shudder and fall to the ground. Then I turn and walk back to the car.

27

I wake not knowing where I am. I lift my head and wince at the shooting pain in my neck. Glancing around, groggy, I realize I'm in a hospital ER waiting room. Alone, apart from the strangers in the other plastic seats in various states of disrepair. I glance down at my bloody shirt. Then I remember. Randy is dead. Blake is dead. Novak and Rex are shot and in surgery.

A door to the left swings open and March comes toward me clutching two coffees in paper cups, her sensible brogues squeaking on the linoleum floor.

"I thought you might need this," she says, holding out a cup. "White, no sugar, and please be careful, it's hot."

It smells wonderful and I take it. "That was thoughtful of you, Laura. Thank you. Have you heard anything?" I'm dreading the worst but have to ask.

"Novak is fine," she says, taking a seat.

I let out a breath. "Oh, that's good news."

"Just a flesh wound. On his shoulder. Close to his heart. The doctors said he was pretty lucky."

"And Rex?"

"Still in surgery. Doctors won't tell me any more than that." She blows on her coffee. "They found Randy Miller's camp site. It looks like he had been hiding out there for days, just waiting. He tried to take the three of them out with a high-powered rifle from the edge of the woods."

I exhale. "God, what a mess."

March's face darkens. "We never thought to plan for that contingency."

"No."

March frowns into her coffee. "But it seems obvious now. Any vigilante could have been hiding out, not just a troubled relative. We were too focused on Rex escaping. We should have considered the possibility and planned for it."

"Don't beat yourself up, Laura. It was a pretty hard thing to foresee."

"Blake is dead, Ms. Kellaway, because of that oversight."

I put my hand on hers. "Not your fault, March."

She gives me a grim nod.

My phone rings. It's Ethan.

"I'd better take this."

I pry myself from the tub seat and move closer to the window where there's more privacy. I get a few worried glances; I guess a pregnant woman covered in blood would ordinarily be cause for alarm.

I answer the phone and Ethan starts talking immediately.

"Oh, Amelia, thank God. I thought...I just woke up and saw the news. They said there had been a shooting. I thought it was you. But you're alive...you're okay? Are you hurt?"

"I'm fine, Ethan. A little shaken up, but fine," I say gently. "I was going to call earlier but I fell asleep at the hospital. I'm so sorry I worried you."

"And the baby?"

"Oh, she's fine. There's nothing to be concerned about there." My voice hitches in my throat and suddenly everything hits me at once. The chaos of the last twenty-four hours. The distressed sound of Ethan's voice. Tears

148

brim and I turn to look out the window so people don't see.

"Please, Ethan, don't be upset."

"I don't know what I'd do without you, Amelia."

"I'm not going anywhere."

"I'm sorry about the fighting," he says.

"Me, too." I sniff.

"Things are going to change. We'll be better. I'm going to be better, more understanding. I promise."

I watch an elderly woman in her Sunday best cross the concourse clutching a bunch of garden daisies in one hand and a string of a dancing Get Well helium balloons in the other.

"Come home, Amelia."

"Soon, darling. I promise."

I turn back to face the waiting room and see March talking with a doctor in scrubs.

"I think the surgeon's here. I have to go."

"Stay safe," he says.

"I will."

When I approach the exhausted-looking surgeon, he removes his blue scrub cap to reveal a shock of red hair and extends his hand.

"Harry Wilson," he says.

"Amelia Kellaway," I reply, taking his hand. "How is he?"

Dr. Wilson rubs the stubble along his jawline. "He was shot in the femoral artery. That's the large artery in the thigh and the main blood supply to the lower limbs. The risk of death is greatest whenever there's injury to the femoral because of blood loss. By the time Mr. Hawkins reached us, he'd lost an estimated four liters—the average male has five to six liters in his body—so you get the picture, serious, very serious. During surgery, I repaired the artery by drafting a section of a vein from his upper leg to reconnect his femoral artery. We also gave him three blood transfusions and his percentages are slowly returning to normal. The short story is, he's likely to make a good recovery."

I'm surprised by the relief I feel. "How long will that take?"

Dr. Wilson looks thoughtful. "Six to eight weeks overall. He should be up on his feet in a few days and able to partake in light exercise."

My mind races. I'm wondering if we can still make the body recovery work.

There's a commotion behind me. I turn to see Sheila Brenton striding toward us. She doesn't look her usual put-together self, and the stylish monochrome suit and expensive leather pumps have been exchanged for faded jeans, a green pullover, and sensible sneakers.

"I came as soon as I could," she says, ashen. "They said there were fatalities."

"The shooter and an FBI agent," I say.

She stands there, breathing. "God." She looks at me. "Novak?"

"He's fine."

She lowers her shoulders. "Thank God." Pausing, she says, "What the hell happened out there?"

"The shooter was one of the victims' brother. Randy Miller," I say. "It seems he just couldn't cope with his loss and wanted revenge."

The governor lets out a long, slow breath. "What a fucking disaster. Has the deceased agent's family been informed yet?"

"No, ma'am," says March.

"I'll do it," says the governor.

"There's really no need for that. The service has people," I say.

"I want to. It's the least I can do. And what about him? That son-of-a-bitch Hawkins?"

I sigh. "Injured but alive. Dr. Wilson was just updating us on his progress."

The surgeon shakes the governor's hand and repeats his update.

"Pity," she mutters, when he finishes.

"Actually, Governor. It could be a blessing," I say, seizing the opportunity. "We managed to recover one body and were close to getting a second when the shooting happened. Rex could still help us."

She looks appalled. "That's absolutely out of the question."

"But Governor, we're so close. Let us finish the job."

Sheila Brenton shakes her head, resolute. "I won't allow it. I should never have permitted this farce to go ahead in the first place."

I push harder. "No one knew this was going to happen. Think of the families."

Her eyes lock on mine. "Two men are dead, Ms. Kellaway. Two more injured. Not to mention the political fallout. This circus is over and it's time you went home."

28

When Rex was eight, he used to hunt bullfrogs down at the ponds in the summer months. A couple of younger kids named Jed and Pete would tag along, too. Down-and-outers like himself with useless good-for-nothing whores of mothers who couldn't give a rat's about what their young'uns got up to.

The three of them would do their frog hunting at night. It was easier that way because you could use your flashlight then. There were several benefits to using a flashlight when frog hunting. First, it helped locate the frogs because just like cats' eyes, frogs' eyes have a foil-like tapetum behind their retinas that reflect and illuminate in the light. Second, shining a light in the frogs' eyes stuns the little sons-of-b's, causing them to freeze on the spot making them easy targets. Third, with a light in their eyes, the slimy suckers can't see you coming.

Some hunters liked to use a bow and arrow, but Rex preferred a rig, a spear-like tool with tines on the end. He fashioned himself a real good one with three-tines, made from steel he found at the junkyard bordering his house. He'd spent hours sharpening the tines against a fragment of grinding stone, and got those tines so sharp that the rig could draw blood by barely skimming your finger.

Rex got pretty good at frog hunting. More than pretty good, as a matter of fact. He could catch up to a dozen or more in a night. Big fat fellas. Some of those sons of guns were sixteen to seventeen inches long. The others he caught were no slouches, either. He loved it out there, knee deep in water, mosquitoes buzzing around his head, the briny smell of the ponds. The other two boys never caught much, and mainly hung at his shoulder, whooping and hollering whenever Rex scored a big one.

Afterward, he'd make a fire and they'd roast the legs on sticks over the flames. It felt good looking across the glowing embers and seeing the two boys chomping and chewing on the bounty he provided for them.

Over time, though, the hunting lost its challenge. It got too easy. The frogs died too quickly. So Rex changed his technique. Instead of killing them instantly by spearing them through the head, he would sink his rig into the lower extremities so as not to kill the frog right away but to simply pin it down. It would squirm there, its little bowed legs lashing out wildly. Then Rex would take his pen knife from his pocket and cut off the limbs one by one, first its hands and feet, then its arms and legs, and finally its head. He would stand back and watch the frog convulse in its last death throes, the cavities of its amputated limbs leaking green blood, the blink of its glistening bulbous eyes gradually getting slower and slower. He did it out of curiosity more than anything else. That first time Jed went as white as a ghost and Peter had cried. What are you blubbering for, it's only a frog, Rex had said.

From time to time Rex did the same thing with bumble bees, trapping them in jam jars, screwing the lids tight, and watching them bounce around the glass until they suffocated.

When he killed frogs or bees, mostly he felt nothing. Which puzzled him. He knew he was supposed to feel some sort of regret or remorse, but he didn't. The only thing he felt was an occasional strange sense of relief. Like his load had gotten a little lighter. Like he could breathe a little easier.

One day things got out of hand. Even Rex had to admit to that. He didn't know what caused him to do it, general frustration at the world, the situation at home, the fight with his mother's boyfriend the night before when he had Rex up against the wall beating the shit out of him. Whatever the precursor, he definitely crossed a line when he went frog hunting that night with Jed and Pete. Instead of the usual pinning down and dissection, Rex simply snatched the frog from the water and squeezed it in his fist until the thing burst in his hand. Pete wet his pants and ran off. Jed was sick in the bushes. But Rex just stood there staring at what was left of the frog, then tossed it in the water and wiped his hand on the grass.

That was the last time Jed and Pete went frog hunting with Rex. It was probably the last time he had any real friends to speak of. Looking back now, it was just as well those two had the good sense to stay away.

Rex turns over in his bunk and stares at the ceiling. Why he is thinking of all this now, he doesn't have a clue. Maybe it was being out there in the woods with the body recovery. Maybe the frog hunting was where it all began. Or maybe he just wants a few of those fat little suckers to squeeze to death right now.

A shooting pain grips his left leg and he winces. Apart from taking short laps around the yard at rec time to keep the blood circulation going, he's spent the last week in his cell with his leg up while the others were on work detail.

Speaking of which, Stan would be back soon with his chattering nonsense about the rights and wrongs of the day. Still, it helps pass the time, and time is all that Rex has left since the body recovery had been called off.

Truth be told, Rex hasn't felt himself since he's been back. Depressed isn't exactly the right word...more like aimless. Like a job he'd set to had been left undone. And that just isn't his nature. He prides himself on always finishing what he starts. He had wanted to help. He truly had. Now there is nothing. Just him and this prison and the walls closing in.

The pain gets him up and moving. He does a few labored laps of the cell and then sits down to check the wound.

"Hey, Rex. You need to see the nurse?"

Rex looks up. It's Bruce doing his usual mail run.

"Morning, Bruce. It's nothing. The dressing's a mess but it's being changed in the morning anyways. How are things with you?"

Bruce grins.

"What is it? You win the lottery or something?"

Bruce pulls a letter from the mail sack and taps it against the bar. "I've got something for you."

Rex looks away. "I don't need another pair of panties, Bruce."

"Your boy wrote you."

Rex stares at Bruce. "My boy?"

"It's from your son. It says so right there on the returnee address. Noah Lee Hawkins. That's him, isn't it?"

Rex's heart pounds. "Yes, it is."

Bruce slips the letter through the bars. Rex takes it and studies the writing and the returnee address.

Bruce gives him a wink. "Thought you'd be pleased. I'll leave you to it then."

After he's gone, Rex lowers himself onto his bunk and stares at the envelope. He slips his finger under the flap and pulls out a letter and photograph. The photograph is of a grown man Rex can only assume is Noah. Noah has his arm slung around a woman's shoulders. A girlfriend or wife. The last time Rex saw Noah he was ten, when he was barely up to Rex's shoulder. The man in the photograph stands proud with his shoulders back and is probably a good head taller than Rex. A strong jawline, too.

Rex places the photograph aside and reads the letter. The writing is barely legible and littered with spelling mistakes, but Rex doesn't care. His boy has reached out. The letter only runs to three paragraphs and Rex skim reads, eager to take it all in. Well, what do you know, he's going to be a granddaddy, isn't that something? His eyes halt on the next sentence. His heart skips a beat. He rereads the sentence twice just to be sure. But he isn't mistaken—Noah is coming to see him.

29

On visiting day Rex wakes early, a full hour before the official 6 a.m. head count. He rolls on his side and looks at Noah's photograph stuck to the wall. It doesn't matter that it's barely visible in the pre-dawn light, Rex has studied it so many times these past few days he knows it by heart. Noah is a chip off the old block, there is no doubt about that. He has the same deep-set blue eyes and square jawline as him. The same colored hair he'd had at Noah's age, and a similar broad-shouldered frame. From the way the boy is standing, it looks like he has a nice manner about him, too. The casual yet protective way that Noah's arm is slung around his woman's shoulders speaks volumes.

Rex takes the photo from the wall and holds it between his fingers and stares at the woman squinting into the sun. Mandy, according to the letter. Plain and wide-hipped, not too pretty. A good choice. The pretty ones get ideas.

Rex thinks back to when he first met Noah's mother in a bar in downtown Portland. He'd seen her around before, at the restaurant near the park where she was a waitress and he was a patron. The night he walked into the bar, their eyes locked in recognition and he asked if he could buy her a drink. He was at an in-between stage, when he was trying to stop with the killings, and he thought if he tried settling down with a good woman it might help. It didn't. In less than a month he was back to it again, and to top it off, eight weeks into the relationship she tells him she's pregnant. By that time, she knew who he was. The oil refinery guy with the big money.

"You don't want this baby any more than I do," she had said. "Twenty grand and I'll get rid of it."

The callousness with which she had delivered those lines had shocked him. But money could do that to a person. Bring out the worst in them, even prompt a mother to murder her own child for a little bit of cash. He'd refused, of course, and sent her on her way, and to be honest he gave no thought about her again until five years later when she turned up on his doorstep with five-year-old Noah in tow. She was strung out on something or the other and wanted money. This time he gave in on the condition he could see the boy from time to time. And for a while there, she kept up her side of the bargain and would dump the boy on Rex a couple of times a year whenever she was passing through Oregon.

He and the boy would go to McDonald's and they would sit there and try to make conversation. It was hard and never got easier with time. Eventually, Noah's mother met someone, a biker, and they moved out east with Noah, and Rex never saw them again. Truth be told, it was a relief. By that time Rex had a lot of other business to contend with.

"Countdown in five minutes, people!" blares the disembodied voice over the PA system.

The day lights come on, and Rex returns the photograph to the wall, gets out of bed, and puts on his day clothes.

He winces. His leg is still sore, especially first thing in the morning. He checks the bandages. No blood has seeped through in the night so the wound must be healing. It still hurts to walk and get around the place, though, and would for some time considering the surgeon had told him it would take up to six months to recover. Rex would just have to persevere and ride out the pain. Last night he'd been thinking that he'd make up his own rehab routine because he sure as hell isn't going get that here. It is especially important that he get back to his regular fitness level and health now that he has reestablished contact with Noah; he doesn't want the boy to think him weak and old.

"Hey, get up, Stan. Sounds like Sheldon's on duty and you know how he gets."

Stan groans and pulls the blanket over his head.

"Come on, my boy. You don't want a ticket."

Stan grumbles beneath the blanket but eventually pulls it aside. The big fat shiner on his left eye has turned completely black. He returned from the shower with it yesterday. When Rex asked what happened, Stan just shrugged. The boy knew better than to snitch, even to Rex. It was just one of those things Stan has to endure every so often. Rex suspects there's more to it than just a black eye, but Stan isn't saying so. Rex saw a pair of Stan's bloody underwear buried in the small trash can under the desk, which made Rex madder than hell, and he wondered at the time whether he should teach Stan how to fight back, or at least defend himself. But the boy would probably only make matters worse. No, Stan is best to stick to his usual strategy—be as useless and harmless as possible. That way, he isn't a threat to anyone and will end up just raped and beaten rather than dead.

"Big day, Rex," says Stan between yawns.

"You bet."

Stan gets off his bunk, grabs his prison-issued sweatshirt from the floor, and pulls it over his head.

"Noah sure is lucky to have a pop like you," he says, bending to slip on his laceless canvas sneakers.

It's not the first time that Stan has said this during the last few days. He has been fussing around Rex ever since Noah's letter arrived. Rex feels sorry for him. Stan never knew his daddy. There would never be any father-son visits for him.

Cell count clears in less than twenty minutes and Rex and Stan are soon merging with the other prisoners in the chow hall. This morning's breakfast is watery oatmeal, a tub of pineapple Jell-O, and an overripe banana.

"You got a bounce in your step today, Rex," says Lionel, the server, a big Mexican man with a thick mop of curly black hair.

"Rex's son is visiting today," says Stan.

"Is that right?" says Lionel, smiling.

"He's coming all the way from Idaho to see him, and Rex is going to be a granddaddy, too."

Lionel looks at Rex. "Well, congratulations, my man. That sure is something."

"Thank you, Lionel."

"Hey, ass-wipes, you're holding up the line."

It's Knepper, three people back in the queue. The big oaf is scowling, causing the swastika tattoo between his eyes to fold in on itself.

"Why don't you keep your big mouth shut, Knepper," says Lionel.

"Why don't you keep your big Mexican dick out of the guacamole, Lionel," says Knepper.

Rex takes his tray from the counter. "My apologies, Knepper. I didn't mean to keep a man from his food."

The last thing Rex wants is an altercation today. Especially not with Sheldon on duty. He wouldn't hesitate to throw them all in solitary for a week if there was any disturbance.

Rex walks up to Knepper and holds out his pineapple Jell-O. "Tell you what, you can have my Jell-O for the inconvenience."

Knepper's eyes drift down to the Jell-O and then back up to Rex's face. "What's the catch?"

"Oh, no catch. Just feeling generous." Rex puts on his friendliest smile. "Go on, it's yours."

Knepper takes it. Inside Rex chuckles to himself. Easy as feeding a monkey in a zoo.

*

The morning crawls by. Rex does his best to distract himself by putting the final touches to his ship-in-a-bottle. All that is required is to connect the last mast to the jigger boom, then hoist the final sail and he's done. It is detailed work that requires a steady hand. The fragile mast is comprised of half a dozen toothpicks stuck together with flour glue, so any sudden movement could cause the thing to break. It takes eight attempts for Rex to attach the mast to the boom and he very nearly gives up. It doesn't help that he can hear Stan behind him, breathing over his shoulder. Finally, Rex gets there and the boom and the mast hold fast.

"Nice one," says Stan.

"Thank you, Stan," says Rex. "I'm a bit off my game today."

The next task is to hoist the sail, the final sail of three. It is a pretty white thing, fashioned from a pair of satin panties that Rex had been sent by one of his fangirls. He takes a breath and eases the loop of thread through the neck of the bottle and tries to slip it onto the end of the

161

mast. But Rex keeps missing it. He growls under his breath in growing frustration.

"Want me to try?" says Stan.

Rex sits back in the chair. "Be my guest."

Stan picks up the tweezers and guides the thread carefully through the neck of the bottle. He pauses there, biting his lip, then slips the loop over the end of the mast and tugs gently on the thread and the sail goes up.

Rex claps a hand on Stan's shoulder. "Well done. You're a natural."

Stan looks up at Rex, beaming. "I did it, didn't I?"

Rex smiles. "You certainly did."

After lunch, Rex wraps up the ship in a crumpled sheet of parchment paper and sits on his bed to wait for the 2 p.m. visiting hours to begin. He forgoes yard time because he doesn't want to risk being late back to his cell. Possibly driven by the latest attack, Stan, bless him, has suddenly gotten it into his head that he needs to do a weights program at what passes for the prison gym. He's there now, leaving Rex alone in the cell with his thoughts.

He has been thinking through how the conversation with Noah would go. Whether he should start out with some sort of apology and whether he should offer him money, especially with a new kid on the way. It occurs to Rex then, he hardly knows anything about Noah at all, not even what he does for a living.

Just before 2 o'clock, Bruce passes his cell and gives him a wink.

"I'll come and get you as soon as your boy arrives," he says.

At a quarter after two, Rex starts to worry. He watches the other prisoners be escorted out of the wing as their visitors arrive. There's only an hour of visiting time to begin with so if Noah is any later, they won't have much time.

At twenty-five past the hour, Stan appears in the doorway, pinked-faced and sweaty. "You're still here," he says, surprised.

"I am."

"Isn't he here yet?"

"What does it look like it, Stan?"

A hurt look flashes across Stan's face. "Sorry, Rex. I didn't mean anything by it."

Rex turns away. "Forget it. It's not your fault."

Stan lowers himself onto his bunk and they sit there in silence as the minutes tick by. At twenty past three Bruce appears.

Rex gets to his feet. "What is it, Bruce? Did something happen to Noah?"

"I'm sorry, Rex. He didn't show."

Stan looks at Rex. "Maybe he had an accident."

Rex studies the package in his hand and starts to unwrap it. "No, Stan, I don't think so." He removes the ship from the brown paper and places it on the desk. "The boy has every right to change his mind if he wants to."

Bending, Rex rests his hands on his knees and peers inside the bottle at the mast and the boom. The join he had glued earlier was coming apart.

"Looks like we got some remedial work to do, Stan."

He glances over his shoulder. Stan and Bruce are staring at him.

"Don't just stand there, Stan, hand me the tweezers, and let's get this thing fixed."

30

The letter arrives a week later. At first, Rex is going to throw it away without opening it. But in the end, he can't bring himself to do that, so he waits until Stan leaves for work detail then reads it in private. The note is short and written in the same chicken scratch as before. Mandy didn't think it was a good idea that I come see you. She's says it's better to let sleeping dogs lie. She's fearful for the baby. Just wanted to let you know. Goodbye and good luck.

Rex reads it twice then puts the letter down. It's a shame the boy has turned out to be so weak. To let his woman call the shots like that. Still, maybe that is Rex's fault. For not being around to show the boy how a real man conducted himself in the world.

Rex digs inside the desk drawer and locates the photograph and the first letter Noah sent. Kneeling on his bed, he reaches over to the shelf that holds the toothpaste, brushes, and safety razors, and retrieves the lighter secreted away in the plastic tumbler. Contraband he exchanged for a week's worth of fruit sometime back. Strictly not allowed, but handy to fuse the bits and pieces of his model together.

He checks outside the cell. Satisfied the coast is clear, he sets the photograph and two letters alight. Pinching them between his fingertips, he holds them over the toilet while they burn, releasing them only when the flames reach his skin. He stares at the dirty remnants floating in the toilet water like scum. Then he pulls the lever and flushes them away.

"What's that smell? You got weed or something?"

It's Knepper. The bulk of his frame filling the doorway.

"You not on work detail?" says Rex.

Knepper holds up his forearm and proudly displays a deep gash that dissects the face of Adolf Hitler in two.

"Impressive," says Rex.

Knepper shrugs and lowers his arm. "I put my arm through a plate glass window in the laundry. Sheldon was pissing me off."

Rex looks at Knepper, considering. "Hey, you want to trade for a favor?"

Knepper's eyes narrow. "What kind of favor?"

Rex turns away and sits down at his desk. "Forget it. You wouldn't be interested."

"Why don't you let me decide that."

"It's nothing. Like I said, forget it. I shouldn't have brought it up."

Knepper doesn't move. "I'm not going anywhere until you tell me."

Rex nods to the ship-in-a-bottle. "See that? Well, it's finished now and I want to start a new one. It would be super handy to have some sort of cutting instrument."

"Cutting instrument?"

"Yeah, you know, like a knife. Or what passes for a knife in this place."

"A knife?"

"How about it? Can you get me one?"

Knepper crosses his arms. "How dumb do you think I am?"

"I don't think you're dumb at all, Knepper. I know you're a man of influence and I got a need to fill, that's all."

"You're setting me up."

Rex shrugs and turns away. "Suit yourself."

Knepper hesitates. "And what do I get in return?"

"Name your price."

Knepper runs his tongue over his teeth and glances around the cell. He starts walking slowly, counterclockwise, lifting things and putting them back down. He stops at the ship-in-a-bottle and picks it up.

Rex shakes his head. "I promised that to Stan."

"What if I said that was my price?"

"I would say no deal because I'm a man of my word and I gave it to Stan already."

Knepper returns the ship to its place. "I don't want your stupid toy, anyway."

He pauses, thinking. A look of realization passes over his features.

"I got it," he says. "What I want is for you to tell me every last detail about what you did to those whores."

Rex studies Knepper's ugly face, the pitted acne-ridden cheeks, the permanent scowl, the glistening lips.

He frowns. "I don't know, Knepper. That's a big ask."

Knepper prods Rex's chest with his finger. "Well, that's my price, ass-wipe. And you gotta tell me everything. Every last detail of what you did to them and what you made them do to you."

Rex pretends to think it over. "It's not an easy thing to talk about."

Knepper exhales. "Then I guess you don't get your shank."

Rex pauses for a suitable length of time. "Okay, if that's your price, I'll do it."

In less than an hour Knepper is back with the makeshift knife. Made of some sort of hard plastic, it's small and sharp and shaped like a feather. Rex wraps it in a T-shirt and slips it under his mattress. He turns to Knepper. The image of Emma Downing flashes into his mind, victim number three. He feels a stirring in his groin.

He smiles at Knepper. "You best take a seat then."

31

Rex looks up at the overcast sky. Twenty minutes until the end of yard time if the weather holds. Any sign of rain and everyone will be taken back to their cells.

"Your move."

Stan signals to the checkerboard laid out on the concrete bench between them. Rex considers the move Stan's just made. A poor choice. But unsurprising. Stan has still not mastered the basics, despite Rex's tutelage. Originally, Rex was going to teach the boy chess but when Stan had difficulty in telling a rook from a pawn, it quickly became apparent that checkers might be a better option.

"I see where you're going with that, Stan. Very smart indeed," says Rex.

Rex pretends to take a long time to contemplate his next move. There's about a dozen different ways he could win the game right now but it is more fun to let Stan do the winning. Eventually Rex makes his move—the worst move possible under the circumstances.

"Your turn, Stan," he says.

Rex looks around while Stan thinks about his next play. This afternoon there's a low-key hum in the yard. Nothing much is going on. No dramas or fights or dustups between the gangs. Everyone's minding their own business for a change.

On the cracked concrete pad, there's the thump, thump, thump of the basketball as the black boys shoot hoops. Close by, some guys are doing a variety of exercises on the rusty outdoor gym equipment. Pull-ups on a set of rings. Ab-work on the ramp. Press-ups on the bars.

Apart from that, everyone is grouped in clusters around the yard, mostly according to specific race gangs. The Nuestra Familia. The Mexican Mafia. The Aryan Brotherhood. The Black Guerrilla Family. The Northern Structure. The Nazi Lowriders. And, finally, the non-domination outliers like Rex and Stan and the old-timers, maybe once Hells Angels or the like, who now just prefer to keep to themselves.

Rex counts the guards. They are a couple down today, which isn't unusual for a Saturday. There's the standard lone guard with the rifle in the watchtower and three more in the yard. Sleepy McPhee is over by the basketball court watching the game. Sheldon is making a nuisance of himself with one of the Hispanic gangs, conducting what looks like an impromptu body search. Bruce is stationed by the main block entrance talking with Pete Steinmann, a notorious self-harmer, who seems more jittery than usual.

Rex feels the shank in his sneaker, positioned parallel to the side of his foot. He knows he cut himself, but that is of minor importance; all that mattered was getting the shank into the yard undetected and he'd succeeded.

He looks over his shoulder. Knepper and his Aryan Brotherhood brethren are close by, near the chain-link fence, no doubt talking shit.

"Your move," says Stan.

Rex returns to the checkerboard, making a big deal to seem impressed by Stan's move.

"Good to see you're putting all that practice to use, Stan," he says.

Rex leans forward and his elbow brushes against the board, sending the checkers clattering to the ground.

"Oh, darn it. I'm sorry, Stan. And you were winning, too."

"No mind, Rex. I'll get them."

Stan kneels at Rex's feet and starts gathering the checkers.

"You know, Stan, you might just be the best friend I ever had."

Stan looks up and smiles and Rex reaches for the shank in his shoe. He wants it to be as quick and painless as possible, so he moves as fast as he can, swinging his arm around Stan's chest and slicing the knife across Stan's throat.

Stan's hands fly up to his neck. He stares at Rex, bewildered, then clambers to his feet, the blood gushing through his fingers. Staggering toward the fence line, he reaches out for Knepper.

"Motherfucker!" says Knepper, jumping out of the way of the spraying blood.

Rex throws the shank on the ground and yells, "Guard! Knepper's got a shank!"

Knepper spins around and stares at Rex, mouth ajar. "What the fuck."

Rex yells again. "Knepper's got a shank!"

Knepper bares his teeth. "Oh, you're gonna die, asshole."

Knepper charges for Rex and they both smash to the ground with a thud. Knepper punches Rex in the face then pivots to grab the shank lying close by. Rex tries to roll away, but he's not quick enough and Knepper plunges the shank into Rex's already wounded leg. Rex cries out and scrambles backward as Knepper goes in for a second round, this time aiming for Rex's chest. Suddenly Sheldon appears and rips Knepper off Rex with a vicious headlock and the shank goes flying. But the reprieve doesn't last long and Sheldon is quickly overpowered when one of the Aryan Brothers gives a war cry and jumps onto Sheldon's back. Seconds later it's all on when the rest of the brothers join in, piling on top of Sheldon to kick the shit out of him. Rex manages to get to his knees and retrieve the shank, slipping it up his sleeve.

Bruce hurries toward him breathlessly.

"You okay, buddy?" says Bruce, crouching down.

"I've been stabbed," Rex gasps. He looks past Bruce. "Looks like the natives are about to blow."

Bruce glances over his shoulder, eyes widening when he sees the other prisoners in the yard running toward them. "Mother of Christ," he utters. He fumbles with his two-way radio. "Comms! Possible riot. I repeat. Possible riot in progress! Over."

"It hurts bad, Bruce," says Rex, tipping his hand to show Bruce the blood.

"Whereabouts?" says Bruce, fumbling with Rex's clothing. "He hit an organ?"

Rex presses the shank into Bruce's side. "Easy."

Bruce tenses. "What are you doing?"

"Listen carefully, Bruce. We're going to cross the yard and head inside and if anyone asks, you're taking me to the infirmary. Once we're clear of the guard, we'll turn right at the kitchen then head to the south side until we get to the parking lot, then I'm out of your hair for good. You do this for me and you won't get hurt. Do we understand each other, my friend?"

171

Bruce stands there, frozen. Sweat has broken out on his top lip.

"Did you hear what I said, Bruce?"

Bruce licks his lips. "Don't do this, Rex."

"It's already done, my friend. Now do I have your cooperation?"

Bruce pauses, then nods. "I'll do what you say."

They cross the yard. In the commotion, the watchtower guard is too busy barking orders into his earpiece to even notice them pass. They reach the entrance to the block, and Bruce quickly unlocks the metal door and they step inside. Guards are running up the corridor, pulling on riot gear.

"The prisoner is injured. He needs the infirmary," says Bruce.

They barely rate a glance and are ushered through without question.

"Well done, Bruce."

They carry on up the corridor and come to the intersection between the different blocks where a guard is stationed behind protective glass. His name is Boris Kowalski. He looks more like an overweight gamer than a prison officer.

Rex glances at Bruce, who's sweating pretty bad. "Nice and easy, Bruce," Rex says. "The infirmary, remember?"

They approach the booth.

Kowalski stands up, agitated. "What the hell's happening out there?"

Bruce shrugs. "Some tiff. Someone bought a shiv out to play and things fired up. This one got a swipe, just taking him to the infirmary, okay?"

"Sure, sure," says Kowalski, buzzing them through.

Rex and Bruce carry on, turning left when they're out of sight of Kowalski.

"Through the first set of doors then into the kitchen storeroom," says Rex.

Bruce does as he's told and they enter the kitchen, empty of people at this time of day. To the left, there's a double-door freezer unit and a large larder to the right where bulk supplies like flour, sugar, and cornmeal are kept. Rex points to the doorway on the other side of the room.

"If I remember correctly, the supply entrance for service vehicles is around to the left and the staff lot is just beyond that, am I right?"

Bruce nods. "Yeah, but the watchtower has eyes on it. There's also a trigger on the door. On the northern side there's a different entrance for the laundry trucks. It's closer to the parking lot and the guys sometime use that entrance on rainy days, even though they're not supposed to. It's swipe-card access only and isn't monitored."

"You wouldn't be fooling me now, would you, Bruce?"

Bruce shakes his head. "I'm no hero, Rex."

"Show me."

They head through the door and go north, making their way to the quiet part of the prison. They reach the exterior door and Bruce digs inside his pocket for his swipe card and uses it to open the door. A gust of cold air hits them. Rex looks around, pleased. There's an empty vehicle bay and the staff lot right next to it, just as Bruce said.

"Which one is yours?" says Rex.

"Over there, in the corner. The yellow Honda."

"Let's go," says Rex.

They hurry down the ramp into the vehicle bay and get inside Bruce's car. Rex glances in the backseat and sees a couple of Walmart bags with what looks like a roll of wrapping paper and some toys.

Bruce sees him looking. "It's my son's birthday tomorrow."

"I remember," says Rex.

"I got him a ship model. Just like yours."

Rex smiles. "That's just swell, Bruce. He's going to love it."

Rex spies a canvas sports bag at his feet. He unzips it and pulls out a blue Knicks hoodie and a pair of tracksuit pants.

"You been hitting the gym, Bruce?"

Wincing in pain, Rex slips out of his prison-issued shirt and pants and pulls on Bruce's clothes. At least three sizes too big but better than nothing. Rex opens the glove box and lets out a whistle when he sees the gun.

"That looks like a nine-millimeter Smith and Wesson to me," he says, taking it.

Bruce looks at him. "You're not planning on hurting folks with that thing, are you, Rex?"

Rex turns the gun over in his hand then tucks it into his waistband. "I have absolutely no intention of doing that, Bruce. It's a tool, that's all. If everyone cooperates, no one gets hurt." He looks out the windshield. "Right, listen up. I'm going to get in the backseat and lie down. This gun is going to be pointed right at your back. You're going to drive up to the checkpoint and tell the man you're knocking off early because you ate some bad chicken. If he puts up a fight, you tell him you're about to puke then and there. If he still puts up a fight, I'm going to shoot him in the head. Got it?"

Bruce wipes the sweat from his forehead. "Yes."

Rex climbs through to the backseat and lies down. "Okay, Bruce, you know what to do."

Bruce starts the engine and drives across the parking lot. When he reaches the gates, he winds down the window.

"Hey, Bruce. Hear you got a brawl going on in there," says the guard.

"Yeah, usual bullshit. Luckily, I've been on the wing all night so I've been kept out of it. I got some stomach thing and I'm heading home early."

There's a pause. "Geez, I'm sorry, Bruce, I can't let you through. We're on standby for lockdown."

"Come on, man. I've been puking my guts out all night and I just want to go home to bed."

"You know I can't do that. Procedure and all."

Bruce groans. "Have pity on me, Marty. It's my son's birthday tomorrow. I need to get clear of this bug."

"Yeah? How old's he going to be?"

"Ten."

"You having a party and what-not?"

"We most definitely are. His mother's probably in the kitchen right now, cooking up a storm. Jesus, don't make me think of food."

There's a moment of silence. "You do look like shit, Bruce. Sweating all over the place..."

"Sweats are the least of it, Marty, let me tell you."

Marty sighs. "I had something like that myself not long ago. Could be something's making the rounds."

"Tell you what, I'll bring you some birthday cake."

"What kind of cake?"

"Chocolate. Tammy does a real good cream cheese frosting, too."

"That sounds nice."

Bruce doesn't say anything, lets Marty think it over.

Finally, Marty exhales. "Go on, Bruce, get outta here."

Rex hears a buzz and the gates slide open with a mechanical grind.

"Thanks, Marty. I appreciate it."

"Just bring the cake, and make it a big chunk, too."

Once they're clear of the prison, Rex sits up and sees the deserted strip of road ahead of them. The sky has darkened overhead and it has just begun to rain.

"Keep going a few miles, Bruce. I'll tell you where to from there."

They travel in silence. About three miles down the road, Rex tells Bruce to pull over. Bruce does as instructed.

He looks at Rex in the rearview. "You gonna kill me now, Rex?"

"Step out of the car, Bruce."

"Can I say goodbye to my family first? Just a text?"

Rex is surprised at how composed Bruce is. "Do as I say, my friend."

Shoulders sagging, Bruce gets out of the car.

Rex does the same and they face each other. "You've been good to me, Bruce. You truly have."

Bruce nods. "No matter what a man has done, he still needs to be treated with dignity."

"I appreciate that, Bruce." Rex raises the gun. "God bless you."

Bruce closes his eyes. Rex looks at him there, the big black man, with a son about to turn ten. He lowers the gun.

"Would you give it thirty minutes, Bruce? Before you make your way back to the prison?"

"I would, Rex. You have my word."

"All right, Bruce. Thank you."

Rex reaches into the backseat and gets the Walmart bags. He hands them to Bruce.

"Tell your boy happy birthday from me."

32

I get up from the sofa to boil the kettle. Reaching for the teabags, I see we're almost out so I scribble a reminder on the shopping list notepad. My eyes skim the other items already written there, some penned in my handwriting, others in Ethan's. Toilet paper. Razors. Chicken thighs. Roma tomatoes. Sardines in Louisiana hot sauce (Ethan's handwriting, not mine). Is this what my life has become? Reduced to the minutiae of everyday domestic life? Making trips to the grocery store? Ridding the shower corners of pink soap scum? Scrubbing the toilet bowl until it gleams?

The kettle screams at me. I remove it from the element and make myself a cup of sweet tea with the second to last tea bag and go to the baby's room. There's wrapping paper and baby gifts in the bassinet and on the white IKEA drawers, dumped there yesterday by Ethan and me after everyone left.

My sister, Becca, had thrown me a baby shower. It was good to see her and my mom and my little nieces and nephews. Even two colleagues from work came. Everyone brought cupcakes and gifts for the baby. I was touched.

Mom and Becca swapped swollen ankle stories from when they were pregnant. They pondered out loud whether my baby would have hair, particularly in light of the fact I had been experiencing heartburn lately. They wondered whether she would look more like me or Ethan, and whether she would be troubled with colic or sleep through the night. I could feel the baby inside me, listening. Taking it all in.

Half of me sat there enjoying it, while the other half was a world away in the Oregon forest, trying to figure out a way to get the governor to change her mind about Rex helping with the search.

It had been ten days since the disastrous body recovery and Sheila Brenton still wouldn't budge. We had tried everything. Novak had even arranged for Blake's grieving mother to speak with her. But it was useless. Sheila Brenton was adamant; the prisoner-assisted search was over.

Yesterday Ethan caught me looking at the photographs of Caitlyn McLellan and Rebecca Kilmore. I had been so lost in thought, I hadn't heard him come through the front door so I didn't have a chance to shut down the computer.

"You forget," he said, kissing the top of my head, "you helped bring twenty-four women home."

Yes, all the other bodies had been located, which was more than a good thing, but Caitlyn and Rebecca were still out there and that was just plain wrong.

Ethan means well, but sometimes I wish he'd be less understanding, less comforting, less the all-around good guy. Sometimes I just wish he would stand alongside me and shake his fist at the sky and hate the world for being so unfair.

After everyone left the baby shower, Ethan and I made love on the living room floor. I'm not sure why, but I was desperate to have him. But I felt dull and blunt at the edges, even as he gasped into my hair. When he was done, he lay on his back and stared at the ceiling.

"Mother earth," he said, smiling.

I lower my cup of tea to the nightstand and begin folding the tiny jumpsuits, bibs, rompers, and bunny-ear onesies and put them away in the drawers in neat little rows. I gather fistfuls of the crumpled, brightly colored wrapping paper and stuff them in the garbage bag.

My cell rings. It's Novak.

"Where are you?" he says.

"Home. Why?"

"You got a piece?"

I frown. "Sure. My Glock."

"Get it out and put bullets in it. I'm on my way."

He hangs up. I look at the phone in my hand, trying to make sense of the call. Then I get moving, going into the living area crossing the floor to the side table where I keep my Glock. I check the chamber. Loaded just as it should be. There's pounding on the door. I check through the keyhole and see Novak and half a dozen others behind him. I open up and they swarm through the house.

Novak glances around, looking this way and that. "You been home long?"

"All day."

"You sure?"

"Of course I'm sure. What's going on?"

He grabs the remote and turns on the TV. I stare at the screen in disbelief. There's a nationwide manhunt for Rex Hawkins. One man is dead.

I look at Novak. "He escaped?"

Novak exhales. "Yeah."

"When?"

"Two hours ago." Novak looks at me and pauses. "He was here."

My blood runs cold. "What do you mean he was here?"

"Outside your apartment."

"You're kidding."

He shakes his head. "We got him on surveillance."

I lower myself into the chair.

Novak crosses the floor and looks out the window. "He was across the street. Near the park."

The men gather in the lounge. They tell Novak the apartment is clear. I feel dread enter my heart like a lead weight. The thought of Rex out there stalking me again is too much to take in.

"Want me to call Ethan?" says Novak.

I shake my head.

He shoots me a smile and looks at my belly. "You look like you're about to pop any day now."

"Two weeks," I say numbly, trying to hide my shaking hands.

His phone rings. He answers and listens. He hangs up and looks at me.

"We got toll information from the Delaware Memorial Bridge. Hawkins drove over it thirty minutes ago. He's still using the car he stole from the prison." He looks at the others. "Let's saddle up. Wilmer, let the local law enforcement know." He looks at me. "Amelia, we gotta go. Lock your doors, keep your gun by your side, and shoot anything that moves."

I get to my feet. "I'm coming with you."

He laughs. "No, you're not."

I grab my coat from the hook. "I'm serious, Novak. No one knows him better than I do. You get into any sort of hostage situation, I need to be there."

"Amelia, don't be ridiculous."

"He listens to me."

"He's armed and dangerous."

"I'm not arguing with you, Novak."

I scribble a note to Ethan and leave it on the table.

Novak sucks in a breath. "That's going to be one pissed-off baby-daddy."

I open the door. "Why don't you let me worry about that?"

33

Rex knows he needs to ditch Bruce's car. Cruising the back streets of Delaware, he looks for somewhere to dump it and for another one to steal. His leg is aching. He'd cut himself more deeply than he'd realized and the tan polyester of the driver's seat is soaked in blood. He should have thought to bring some medication. It was a stupid oversight and an unnecessary distraction from having a clear head.

Rex enters a residential area, peering out the window as he drives. It's getting dark and people are beginning to draw their curtains. Others don't and Rex can see right into their houses. Some are eating dinner at tables. Others are sitting on sofas in front of flickering screens.

It makes him think of Amelia. He had taken a risk going to her apartment. He isn't sure why he went. Whether, at the back of his mind, he was planning on taking her. Maybe he just wanted to say goodbye. It is going to be a very long time before he will see her again.

Rex has three possible routes out of the country. During his years on the run, he'd stashed exit kits in bus lockers in North Dakota, Texas, and Florida. The kits contained false passports, credit cards, clothes, a burner phone, and more than enough cash to get him the hell out of dodge. The North Dakota route involved crossing the border into Manitoba and then, depending on circumstances, boarding a ship from Canada and disappearing somewhere in Eastern Europe. The Texas route would see him cross the border into Mexico then boarding the train to Guatemala and making a life for himself in one of the inland villages. The final Florida route, on the other hand, required chartering a boat from a captain who doesn't ask too many questions and fleeing to Puerto Rico. From there he would vanish into one of the Caribbean islands or continue on to Australia.

He settles on the Florida plan. It makes the most sense. It's the closest, plus Rex knows Florida well, having spent a summer there back when he was on the run the first time.

But before any of that's possible, he needs a new vehicle. Rex circles the block again but can't find anything. He tries his luck at the nearby suburban shopping area, where there's a rundown strip mall and a few shops. He enters the parking lot, selecting the space furthest from the entrance. Keeping the engine running, he looks around for an easy target. He needs a make and model he's familiar with, like a Ford or Chevrolet. Nothing too conspicuous or late model, given the probability of alarms and keyless entry. But there doesn't appear to anything suitable.

He glances at the clock on the dash. It's a quarter after seven. He's been in Delaware way too long and it's making him jittery. Just then a woman appears in the doorway of a pain clinic. She crosses the lot and heads for a beat-up silver Mazda hatchback two vehicles away from Rex.

He glances around to make sure the rest of the lot is empty and slips out of the driver's seat. The woman's distracted as she digs inside her purse for her keys and doesn't see him coming up behind her. When she bends to put the key in the lock, he darts his arm out and claps his hand over her mouth. She screams into his palm. Her scream is thick and wet and full of fear. Then she does something he doesn't expect. She bites him. Hard, between the webbing of his forefinger and thumb. He chokes back a yell and punches her in the head. She tries to run but he grabs her.

"What the fuck, asshole?" she spits, struggling against him.

He points the gun at her.

"Get in," he says, gesturing to the driver's seat.

"Fuck you."

He presses the gun under her chin. "I said get in."

"Son of a bitch," she says through gritted teeth.

She has guts. He'll give her that. Not many women would sass a man about to blow their head off. She slides into the driver's seat and Rex gets in the back. There's crap everywhere. Fast food wrappers. A booster seat. His shoes stick to what looks like an ice cream wrapper on the floor.

"What do you want?" she says.

"Where do you live?"

Her eyes widen. "Oh, no way."

"I need a change of clothes. A clean bandage. Painkillers."

She shakes her head. "Not my problem, asshole."

She's pretty in a tired sort of way. Not like the fresh-faced women about to take on the physical challenge of a trek or hike. Her blond hair is pulled back in a ponytail and dark at the roots, and her waxy skin looks like it never sees enough of the sun. She turns around and looks at him.

He waves his gun at her. "Eyes front."

"Don't tell me what to do."

"Start the car. I'm not going to hurt you if you do as you're told."

She pulls a face. "You expect me to believe that?"

"You best pay attention to the fact that I got a gun pointed at you. Don't make this more trouble than it's worth."

She stares at him for a while longer then turns around and starts the car.

"You strung out?" she says, angling the Mazda from the lot and turning left.

He doesn't say anything.

"Just because I'm a nurse doesn't mean I got any drugs."

"I don't want drugs. Just painkillers."

"What for? Your leg? You get shot or something? You look a bit old to be a gangbanger."

"Stop talking."

She purses her lips and mutters something under her breath. She takes a right and heads four blocks north.

"How far is it?" he says.

"An hour or thereabouts."

He frowns. "An hour?"

"Hey, housing's not cheap in Delaware. Everyone says Delaware's a reasonably priced place to live but those fools don't know what they're talking about. You want to live here on a limited income you have to travel."

"An hour's too long," he says.

"You want me to pull over and let you out, I will, asshole."

He considers this. "Keep driving," he says.

34

It's late by the time Novak and I get to the Delaware River and Bay Traffic Authority. We are ushered into the control ops room with wall-to-wall CCTV cameras.

"Everything's live-streamed these days," explains Brian Murphy, the Traffic Area manager. "Anyone can watch online, choose to delay their journey if their route is too congested." He punches a few buttons and taps the keyboard. "Everything is recorded on a continuous loop. But there's only so much space so once the hard drive has been exhausted, it starts recording new footage over the old stuff." He brings up a still image. "We managed to pull this in time though. Once the alert on the prisoner was put out, we started running number plate recognition software and we got him."

I stare at the screen. The back of the modest red Honda looks so innocent.

"How do we know it's him in there?" I say. "He may have ditched the car and someone else took the opportunity to steal it."

Brian shoots me a smile. "I thought you might ask that. There's CCTV on the bridge. They were having issues with suicides awhile back so they installed two cameras at various vantage points." He taps the keyboard again and the screen comes to life with moving footage. "Keep watching."

The red Honda comes into view. All of a sudden there's a clear shot of the driver's side, Rex Hawkins at the wheel.

"Nice work," says Novak.

The Honda crosses the bridge and continues up the road.

Brian looks at us. "We alerted police as soon as we identified the plate, but he was gone by the time the patrol cars got there. Sorry, folks."

I look at the time stamp. Four hours ago. Novak follows my train of thought.

"We don't know for sure he has left the area," he says.

"Come on, Novak. Why would he stick around?"

He shrugs. "He could have local associates helping him."

I shake my head. "Rex works alone. He doesn't trust anyone. He'll have a plan, probably formed a long time ago."

Novak's phone rings. He listens. He hangs up, smiling.

"Are you going to make me guess?" I say.

"They found the Honda."

35

Just as the panic clinic nurse had said, it takes over an hour to reach the ugly block of orange brick rental units where she lives. Thankfully, she managed to keep that smart mouth of hers shut for the duration of the journey, although she maintained the scowl on her face for the entire time. Rex wondered if she'd be so ornery if she knew who he really was.

She pulls into a small parking area adjacent to the ground floor and turns off the engine. Rex looks out the window. It's dark and quiet and no one is around.

"Now what?" she says.

"We go inside."

She hesitates. "What if I go get you the stuff and bring it back it back down?"

"How stupid do you think I am?" he says.

A flash of vulnerability plays across her face. "It's just that…it's my home."

Rex looks at her. "What's your name, sweetheart?"

"Jackie."

"I'll be gone before you know it, Jackie, and your life will be back to normal. How does that sound?"

"I don't have much of a choice, do I," she grumbles.

She gets out and Rex follows.

"Nice and slow," he says, sticking the gun in her side.

They cross the cracked concourse and enter the building.

"We gotta use the stairs," says Jackie. "The elevator is out."

Rex feels his leg ache. "How many floors?"

Jackie looks over her shoulder at him, smiling. "Four."

They enter the door to the stairwell. Lingering at the bottom, there's a couple of wannabe gangster types, probably not a day over fourteen, roughhousing and chugging on a bottle of something in a paper bag.

"Nice and easy," Rex says quietly, slipping the gun into the pocket of his hoodie. "Remember, no one needs to get hurt."

But Jackie isn't listening. Instead she's stomping over to the boys and clipping one of them around the back of the head.

"Simon Kitteridge, you get on home before I tell your momma what you've been doing." She grabs the bottle in the paper bag. "And you won't be needing this anymore."

"Hey," Simon says. "Give that back."

"I will do no such thing," she says, tipping it out on the stairs.

She glares at the other boy. "And you, you good for nothing piece of shit, don't you come around here and lead poor Simon astray. He's a good boy. He's going make something of himself, not like you. Now get the fuck outta here."

The boy rocks on his heels as if he might strike her.

Jackie leans in. "Oh, you want a piece of me?"

The boy backs down, uttering curse words under his breath.

"Later, G," he says to his friend, sauntering out the door.

"Thanks a lot, Jackie," says Simon, bitterly.

"You shouldn't be hanging around with trash like that."

Simon scowls at her. "Bitch."

He turns and lopes up one flight of stairs, taking the first door at the top.

"That was stupid," says Rex.

"Was it?"

She climbs the stairs without looking back.

When they reach the door to her apartment, Rex is breathless. He feels a little dizzy, too. The quicker he gets some painkillers into his system the better. Jackie fumbles in her handbag for her keys.

"Quit stalling," says Rex.

"I'm not stalling. You don't know how crowded a woman's handbag can get," she snaps.

The door next to Jackie's apartment opens. An old lady dressed in her night clothes peers out.

She squints at Jackie then Rex. "Hello, dear. You got a guest?"

"Evening, Mrs. Martinez. How are you? He's just an acquaintance picking something up from my apartment. He'll be on his way soon. Say, you not alone in there, are you? I thought John-John was supposed to be looking after you."

The woman's eyes grow cloudy and she reaches up to the throat of her dressing gown, frowning. "Was he?"

Jackie tuts. "That son-of-a-bitch let you down again? Never mind, Mrs. Martinez, I'll come by and check on you later myself. You go on in now. Get yourself some sleep."

"Is John-John here?" says the old woman, bewildered.

Jackie softens her voice. "No, Mrs. Martinez, but I'm sure he'll be here in a bit. I'll come by soon, now shut the door and go to bed."

"Okay, dear. That would be lovely," she says, closing the door.

"Who's John-John?" asks Rex.

Jackie scowls. "Her free-loading, loser, son-of-a-bitch middle-aged son, that's all. She's got Alzheimer's and he's supposed to be helping her but he's helping himself to her bank account instead."

Finally, she pulls the keys from her purse and opens the door to her apartment. She turns around to Rex, pressing her fingers to her lips. He looks past her and sees two young children asleep on a pull-out sofa on the floor, a toddler and an older girl about nine. The apartment is tiny. No separate bedroom, just the living area where the children are sleeping and a small galley kitchen next to that. She gestures for Rex to follow her and they cross the floor and enter the bathroom.

After shutting the door, she digs inside the medicine cabinet and takes out a bottle of Advil.

Rex isn't impressed. "Haven't you got anything stronger? Vicodin or something similar?"

"Like I said before, just because I'm a nurse doesn't mean I got a pharmacy."

She dumps the bottle in his palm. He shakes out four and turns on the faucet, bending to swallow the tablets down with the water. Standing, he wipes his mouth with the back of his hand.

"I need you to take a look at my leg."

Exhaling in a huff, she puts down the toilet seat and points to it.

"Take off your pants," she says.

She stands there with her arms folded as he removes his track pants and lowers himself onto the seat. Her eyes drop to the sticky mess of congealed blood covering his thigh, then her gaze continues downward, stopping at his sneakers where there's an Aken Correctional stamp on the

192

tongue of the shoe. She meets his eyes but says nothing. Turning to the medicine cabinet, she pulls out a bottle of iodine and a tube of antiseptic cream. She rinses the wound with a washcloth and applies some iodine.

"You need stiches," she says. She gets to her feet. "Wait here."

She disappears out the bathroom door before he can stop her, and she returns a few minutes later with a torn bedsheet and some needle and thread.

"It's gonna hurt, I'm not gonna lie," she says, squinting as she guides the thread through the eye of the needle. She kneels down and pinches either side of the wound together.

She looks at him, pausing. "Okay?"

He nods.

"Take a breath."

She pushes the needle into his flesh and he winces.

"Where's their daddy?" he says.

"I'll let you know when I find out."

"You leave them here while you work?"

"You judging me?" she says.

"It must be hard," he says.

She finishes the last stitch and applies some antiseptic cream. Then she tears strips from the floral sheet.

"This is the best I got."

"It's fine."

She wraps the strips around his leg, then slaps her hands on her thighs and stands. "Okay, that's it."

He pulls up his pants.

"I take it we're done here?" she says. "I've been up all night and I need to get some sleep before those two wake up."

"You got food?"

She pauses, annoyed. "Wait here."

She disappears and comes back a few minutes later with a budget loaf of white bread, a half-eaten jar of peanut butter, and a knife. She slaps peanut butter onto two slices of bread and hands it to him.

"Thanks," he says, taking a bite.

She looks at him while he eats. "I've had my troubles, too," she says. "In the past. It was those two out there that made me get my shit together."

"You're a good mother," he says, chewing. "I can tell."

"I try to be. These days at least."

"I'm going to take your car."

She nods. "Figures."

"I won't wreck it. I'll dump it in a McDonald's parking lot. The police will pick it up and you'll get it back in one piece."

"Whatever you say."

He stops chewing and looks at her. "Why don't you come with me?"

"What?"

"I guess you worked out that people are looking for me. It's hard to drive with my leg the way it is. I would pay you. We'd be doing each other a favor."

"A favor."

They fall silent.

"Where?" she says.

"Florida."

She raises her eyebrows. "Florida's a long way."

"Like I said, I would pay you for your time."

"How much?"

"Ten thousand dollars."

She laughs. "Yeah, right."

"I mean it. I'll give you ten thousand if you drive me to Florida."

"I don't see no money on you."

He shrugs. "Why don't you let me worry about that."

Her eyes narrow. "You rob a bank or something?"

"I could just make you. I could just point this gun at you and force you to go. But the choice is yours, Jackie."

He turns to wash his hands in the sink.

She stands there staring at him. "You're not fooling me? You'd really give me ten thousand dollars for driving you to Florida?"

He straightens up and looks at her. "I would."

She looks at the floor, thinking. She lifts her head. "Okay, I'll do it." She looks over her shoulder, into the apartment. "But those two gotta come, too."

36

The red Honda sits eerily alone in the empty lot near the small grass verge like a luckless moocher who's been caught doing something it shouldn't have. Three patrol cars surround it, their lights flashing red and blue in silence, an indication the situation is serious but not quite an emergency. A long strip of yellow police tape has sectioned off the area, and a few members of the public have gathered behind it. Nightcrawler types, possibly a few homeless people, and a woman walking a dog.

As we pull into the lot, I note the eight stores adjacent to the car park. A dollar store. A pain clinic. A pawn shop. A Best Buy. A 24/7 mini mart. The other two premises have For Lease signs in the window. Given the late hour, all the stores are closed, except for the mini mart and a gas station across the road.

I turn to Novak as he cuts the engine. "What's your take?" I say, looking out the windshield.

He shrugs. "He could've come for supplies, got spooked, ran off."

"If that was the case, he would've parked closer to the store instead of way back here."

"You got a point."

I pause. "He was looking for another car."

There's a knock on my window. It's a woman. Mid-fifties. Serious. Attractive. Dressed in a black puffer jacket. There's a detective's badge on a beaded chain around her neck. Novak and I get out.

She extends her hand. "Detective Janet Tibs. FBI, I take it?"

I nod and take her hand. "Amelia Kellaway, nice to meet you."

She turns to Novak and shakes his.

I note the gleam in his eyes. "Steve," he says, flashing her a smile.

Detective Tibs plants her hands on her hips and nods toward the Honda. "We got a forensic guy in there now scraping for evidence."

"Find anything yet?" says Novak. "A map? A detailed getaway plan?"

I can't believe Novak is flirting at time like this. Detective Tibs shoots me a glance and I keep my face neutral.

"Mind if I take a look?" I say.

"Go ahead."

I duck under the police tape and approach the Honda. There's a forensic guy in a paper Tyvek suit bent over the trunk, examining the contents. I sidestep him and circle the vehicle. No signs of any recent accidents or damage. No mud or other flora on the tires or the undercarriage to indicate he's gone off road. I peer into the driver's seat, see a large blood stain.

"That's got to be at least two liters," says Novak, peering over my shoulder.

"Do you think it's his?" I say.

"More than likely." Novak nods. "In the ruse to get out of the prison, he got stabbed."

"With an injury like that he can't have gotten far." I look at Detective Tibs. "Anything from the hospitals?"

She shakes her head. "No admissions matching his description."

I stand there, thinking. "He came here to steal a car," I say, finally.

The baby kicks me and I double over.

"You okay?" says Novak.

"Give me a minute," I say, winded.

Novak lowers his voice. "Listen, we could find you a motel or something. You could rest up for a bit."

"Forget it, Novak. I'm fine."

The discomfort passes and I turn to Detective Tibs. "Are you pulling the surveillance?"

She nods. "We're arranging that now."

I glance at the stores. We'll be lucky if any of the cameras reach this far into the lot. I stand there, feeling the breeze, listening to the whoosh of cars on the main thoroughfare, tasting the bitter exhaust fumes.

"Anyone report a car stolen from here?" I ask.

Detective Tibs shakes her head.

"You would think that if he had stolen a car, someone would have reported it by now," I say.

Novak looks at me, curious. "What's your thinking, Amelia?"

I take a breath. "He hasn't just stolen a car, he's kidnapped someone."

37

Jackie bundles her sleeping kids into the Mazda. She's a good mom, Rex thinks as she buckles them in. Earlier she'd insisted on bringing some supplies with them on the journey and had dashed around the apartment grabbing diapers and wet wipes and some such things, explaining that the boy still wore diapers. She'd even brought snacks for them. For later. String cheese and mini packs of Doritos for Jeb the three-year old, and a bag of oatmeal cookies for Daisy, the nine-year-old. Jackie was excited, he could tell. It was sweet.

"Fifteen hours is a long way to drive," she'd said, stuffing the last of the gear into the bag. "After I drop you off, the kids and I will need to stay overnight in Florida to get some sleep before we head back. I won't be able to go there and back in one go…"

"Sounds sensible," Rex had said. "So, you got everything you need?"

She shouldered the bag and glanced around the tiny apartment. "I think so."

"We best get going then."

It's 2 a.m. by the time they pull away from the complex. It's a cold, dark night and there's no one around, and apart from a street cleaner truck with its flashing golden lights, there's barely any traffic on the road as they head south into downtown Claymont.

"I take it we're going the I-95 route?" she says. "Through North Carolina and Georgia?"

Rex nods. "That's the one."

"Okay, good. How's your leg?" she says, fiddling with the A/C to clear the fog in the windshield.

"Better. Thank you, Jackie."

She nods, satisfied. "Glad to be of service."

"You're a good nurse."

"I wanted to be a doctor."

"Why didn't you then?"

She laughs. "People like me don't become doctors."

"You still could. You're young enough."

"Seriously? With those two?" She shakes her head. "No way. My fate is sealed."

"You got plans for the money?"

"I'm thinking on it. Pay a few bills, put some away for a rainy day."

Rex studies her profile. "When was the last time you did something nice for yourself? Got your hair done? Bought a pretty dress from a nice store?"

She tuts. "Those days are long gone."

"Well, you're not ugly. You could get yourself a man to look after you."

"Who says I want one?"

Rex glances in the backseat at the sleeping children. "Some men like a readymade family."

"Me and my kids get along just fine without a man."

"You got no family who helps you out?"

When she doesn't answer, he leaves well enough alone. He looks out the window as they pass through the Claymont town center. Rex has been here before twice, once at Christmastime when the locals were having their Claymont Christmas Parade, the other in summer when he was passing through on his way north.

"We need to make a stop," he says.

She frowns. "Where?"

"We have to pick up a package."

Her eyes narrow. "What package? I don't want nothing to do with no drugs."

Rex raises his hands. "No drugs, I swear."

"What then?"

"Cash...Some other items. You need to collect it for me."

They stop on a red at the traffic lights. A patrol car pulls up in the lane beside them.

Jackie stiffens.

"Easy now," says Rex.

Jackie keeps her eyes straight ahead. "Why don't you do it?"

He shakes his head. "Too risky."

The light turns green and she pulls away. The cop goes right.

She taps the steering wheel. "I don't like this."

"You want to get paid, don't you?"

"You promise that's all it is? No guns or anything?"

"No guns, I promise you. Turn right at the corner up here then pull into the bus station and park."

She does as instructed and cuts the engine.

He opens the glove box and feels around. "You got a pen or something? I need to give you a code."

"Use this," she says, bringing up the notes function on her mobile phone.

Rex taps in the number five-seven-three-one and hands it back.

"Inside there's a bunch of self-serve lockers around to the right. You punch in that code. Open the locker. Take the bag. Bring it back. Got it?"

She licks her lip and nods.

"There's nothing to be afraid of," he says. "You're not doing anything wrong. Just getting a bag from a locker."

"What if I'm stopped?"

"Who would stop you?"

"I don't know. The cops could be onto you or something. I'll be aiding and abetting."

He looks out the windshield at the bus station. "Don't overthink it, Jackie. Just get the bag and bring it back."

She glances into the backseat and looks at her children.

"They'll be fine," he says. He pauses. "Just make sure you come back."

She looks at him in disgust. "What kind of mother do you think I am?"

Then she gets out of the car and goes inside.

38

The gas station attendant from across the strip mall is a pale-looking kid around twenty. According to the name badge pinned to the breast pocket of the gray shirt that doesn't quite fit, his name is Tobias Luther. Chubby with a wispy beard, Tobias Luther blinks rapidly as he listens to Detective Tibs explain that we want the security footage from the last eight hours.

"I'll need to call head office first," says Tobias.

Novak lets out an impatient sigh. "Listen, kid, you don't need permission from head office. You have our permission. There's a crime currently in commission and we need that footage right now. It's a matter of life and death. Understand?"

Tobias Luther goes red. "Yes sir, I understand, but that's not what I mean. All our surveillance is routed through the head office cloud. We can't access it down here without a proper code. I just gotta contact the guy and get the code."

Novak washes his face in frustration. "Then you better call him, hadn't you?"

"Take it easy, Novak," I say. "I think Tobias is doing his best." I smile at the boy. "Go ahead, Tobias. If you could make your call and get us that code as quickly as you can, we'd appreciate it."

"Yes, ma'am." Tobias nods, disappearing out the back.

Novak digs inside his pocket and puts a five-dollar bill on the counter. He selects a Hershey's bar from the rack, unwraps it, and chomps. The cloying smell of chocolate reaches me and I begin to feel sick. He offers me and Detective Nibs some.

"I'll pass," I say.

Detective Tibs does the same, turning instead to look out the window at the abandoned Honda across the road.

"Let's hope there's something on the surveillance," she says.

"Amen to that," says Novak, chewing.

Given it was the middle of the night, tracking down the managers from the strip mall stores to access their surveillance hadn't proved easy. It was Novak who had the bright idea that the gas station surveillance might hold the key to what we were looking for. The camera pointed to the rear exit of the parking lot and, depending on its vantage point, potentially captured the spot where Rex abandoned the Honda.

Suddenly my belly squeezes in a painful cramp. I bite my lip, fighting to maintain my composure.

But Detective Tibs catches it. "You okay?"

I plant a smile on my face. "The baby's just in an uncomfortable position."

But it could be more than that. It could be a contraction.

Detective Tibs laughs lightly. "I remember those days."

"Oh, you have children?" I say, finding it difficult to imagine this stern woman as a mother.

She nods, smiling. "Two. Boy and girl. Both with families of their own now." She eyes my belly. "Your first?"

"Yep, and a surprise one at that," I say, rolling my eyes.

There's another twinge low in my belly. I keep my face passive. "If you'll excuse me, Detective Tibs, I'll be back in a moment."

"Bathroom?" says Detective Tib.

"She's like a tap," says Novak, chewing. "I've never seen anything like it."

I ignore him and cross the floor to the bathroom down the back of the store. Once inside, I take a seat in the only stall and look at my watch and try to remember how long ago I felt the earlier cramp. Forty-five minutes? An hour?

I place my hand on my belly. "You settle down in there, daughter. Mama's got work to do."

It's probably just Braxton Hicks. Sandy Liu warned me about them. Sometimes they could go on for days as the body begins to prepare for labor. I stand up. I'll keep an eye on them. Any increase in strength and frequency and I'll do something then. But for now, it's back to work.

My phone rings. It's Ethan. God. I consider letting it pass to voicemail but I need to face the music at some point.

I take a breath and I answer. "Honey, I know you're upset but I didn't have a choice—"

"Are you crazy, Amelia? Do you seriously think it's okay to be chasing down an escaped prisoner in your condition?"

I swallow. I've never heard him so angry. "We think he took someone," I say. "A woman."

"I don't care. Rex Hawkins isn't your responsibility anymore."

"I'm with Novak and a local detective. I'm perfectly safe."

"This isn't just about you anymore, Amelia. It's about the safety of our child."

"Hey, don't imply that I don't care about my baby."

"That's the thing, Amelia. She's not just your baby. She's my baby, too, and right now I'm concerned about any future she might have if your current actions are any indication of your mothering skills."

I'm stung. "Ethan."

I hear him breathing. "I'm just about done with this, Amelia."

"What are you saying? You want out?" I blink back tears.

"Right now, yes. That's exactly what I want."

*

When I emerge from the bathroom, I hope my face isn't too blotchy from crying. I did my best with the cold tap water and paper towels but I doubt it was enough. I tell myself that Ethan doesn't really mean it. This will blow over, just like the other times. And how dare he say I'm not a good mother. That simply wasn't true. I'm trying, really trying. Tears spring again and I swallow them down. How I hate this, all this fighting.

When I reach the front counter, the others are nowhere to be seen. Eventually, I find them in the staff only area, bent over a laptop, Tobias at the keyboard.

Novak looks over his shoulder at me. "Everything all right?"

"I'm fine."

He stares at me for a beat then lets it drop.

"Stop right there," says Detective Tibs, sweeping the dark fringe from her eyes. "Okay, play it back."

We watch the Honda pull into the parking lot. The car is too far away to see the driver.

"Keep going," says Novak.

We continue to watch. The Honda stays put. No one gets out.

"Speed it up," says Novak.

Tobias increases the speed to 1.5x. Twenty minutes flick by. Then forty. We see a woman walk into frame and approach a silver Mazda, two cars away from the red Honda.

"Slow down," says Novak. Tobias does.

The woman pauses at the driver's side of the Mazda and digs through her purse. There's movement from the Honda. A man steps out of the shadows. It's Rex. I feel a chill go up my spine.

I glance at Novak. He meets my eyes. "Looks like you were right," he says.

I nod grimly and we watch as the woman extracts the keys from her bag and bends to insert them into the lock, completely unaware of Rex coming up behind her. Rex puts his hand around her mouth and she jolts upright. The look of sheer terror on her face is hard to take, and I have to avert my eyes and take a breath. When I look back, the woman is struggling so hard that for one moment I think there's a chance she might get away. My heart sinks when I see Rex pull out a gun and force her into the car. Less than twenty seconds later they drive out of the lot, turning left on to the main road.

Novak looks at Detective Tibs. "You get the plate?"

She's already writing it down on her hand. She turns away to make the phone call.

Novak places a hand on Tobias's shoulder. "You did great, kid."

Tobias blinks at us. "You think the lady's going to be all right?"

Novak exhales. "You believe in God, kid?"

"Yes, sir."

Novak nods. "Me, too. I'll be saying a prayer and it might help if you did, too."

39

The Mazda belongs to one Jacqueline Patricia Simons. Age thirty-six. Occupation, nurse. Two children. No arrests. According to police records, Jacqueline Simons filed some complaints of domestic violence some time back. Apparently, she had an ex-husband with a nasty temper that landed her in the hospital with a broken jaw. That was three years ago. Since then she has worked at the pain clinic in the strip mall where her car was taken.

According to her driver's license, Jacqueline lives in an apartment in Claymont so we waste no time and head there. With his injury, it is always possible Rex has decided to lay low rather than continue out of state.

All the worst things tumble through my mind as we race through the streets. I can't believe this is happening again. More innocent victims. More broken lives.

"Novak, we have to find her," I say.

"I know."

He looks as stricken as me. The baby gives me a thump and I feel my belly contract deep and low. I grip the armrest and breathe through my nose. Oh God, I want to groan so bad. But I don't. Instead I grit my teeth and count the seconds until the worst passes and it does and thankfully Novak doesn't notice. I'm getting worried. That's three in the last hour and a half.

When we reach the apartment complex, a patrol car and Detective Tibs are already there, parked discreetly behind a couple of fast food joints across the road. We pull in behind and get out.

"Any sign of the Mazda?" says Novak.

Detective Tibs shakes her head. "None. But that doesn't mean he hasn't hidden it some place around here to throw us off."

Novak looks over his shoulder at the apartment block. "Okay, here's the situation. They may or may not be in there so here's what we're going to do. We don't want the natives getting restless so we're going to do this with a minimum of fuss. Tibs, you come with me and we go knock on the door, easy-like. Anyone stops us on the way, we're making inquiries, that's it—folks around here are probably used to seeing law enforcement from time to time so that shouldn't raise any red flags. Like I said, we knock on the door and we wait. We'll get a feel for whether anyone's inside."

"I'm coming with you," I say.

"Out of the question," states Novak.

Detective Tibs looks at me. "He's right, Amelia. It's far too risky. Quite frankly, you'd be a liability if we have to exit the building quickly."

I don't like it, but I know it's true. "Promise me you'll come and get me if he asks for me. I'm the best option for getting him to surrender."

Novak and Detective Tibs agree and leave me to head across the road. I watch them go inside, fighting a growing sense of dread.

Ten long minutes later, Novak appears in the entrance doorway and shakes his head. I feel a strange sense of disappointment. Novak gestures me over.

"Anything?" I say when I reach him.

"No one's inside. Tibs and her team are going through the apartment now to see if they can find anything to see where they went." He glances at the stairs. "The elevator's out. You want to stay here? I'll fill you in later?"

I look at him and say nothing.

He nods. "Thought so. Don't say I didn't offer."

I follow him up, doing my best not to show the effort it's taking. Even so, I'm forced to pause for breath at least every fourth step because it's not only my useless foot I have to contend with, the ever-increasing weight in my belly is making me feel even more winded than normal.

Eventually, we reach the tiny apartment. Tibs and her officers are sweeping the rooms. I take a look around. It's clear Rex was here and had left in a hurry. I note the bloody rags in the bathroom. The open set of drawers in the living area, half-empty and missing clothes.

I bend to pick up a toy truck. "What about the kids?" I say.

Detective Tibs draws her eyebrows together. "We just spoke with the ex-husband on the phone. He says he hasn't seen them for over a year."

Novak growls in frustration. "Now we got three hostages instead of one, two of them little kids."

Detective Tib's phone rings. She steps outside to take the call.

"Now what?" I say.

Novak runs his hands over his face. "Put out a BOLO. Do an AMBER alert. Media conference…" He exhales. "It's gonna be a goddamn circus."

Detective Tibs comes back in. The color has leached from her face.

"What is it?" says Novak.

"They found a body. They think it might be Jacqueline Simons."

40

She takes a long time. Longer than is strictly necessary, Rex thinks. There's not too many people about at this early hour. Just a few, sleepily wandering through the bus station doors, bags slung over their shoulders. So she can't use that as an excuse.

In the backseat, the young ones are beginning to stir. The toddler starts crying. Rex turns to look.

"Hush now, your momma's gonna be right back."

But even as he says it, he wonders if it might not be true. There was an awful lot of cash in that bag. Enough to start a new life.

The nine-year-old stares at him with those deep hazel eyes of hers.

"Daisy, isn't it?" he says.

She just looks at him and says nothing.

"That's fine," he says, smiling. "You've got every right not to talk to me."

The toddler is getting more worked up and begins to howl.

"How about you tend to your little brother for me?" says Rex. "Would you mind doing that, Daisy?"

The girl pulls the toddler from his booster seat and holds him close. She kisses the top of his head and he quiets down immediately.

"Good girl."

Rex turns around to see Jackie walking toward the car carrying his duffel bag. She gets in and dumps the bag in his lap.

"Sorry," she says. "I had to go to the bathroom, then the code wouldn't work."

"What do you mean the code wouldn't work?"

She shakes her head. "I was nervous. I got the wrong locker at first."

He looks inside the bag. Everything's there. "You didn't talk to anyone?"

She frowns. "Of course not."

He nods, satisfied. No harm done. She completed what was required of her and now they can go.

Jackie turns to her kids. Sees the young one out of his seat. "Everything okay, Daisy?"

"Oh, everything's fine. Isn't that right, Daisy?" says Rex. The girl nods.

Rex says, "Why don't you go ahead and put your little brother back in his seat?" He turns to Jackie. "Let's hit the road. I want to get on the 1-95 before daybreak."

*

They make good time and reach the city limits just as the sun is beginning to rise. Traffic on the I-95 is relatively quiet and the steady hum of the tires against the asphalt makes Rex feel sleepy. He shuts his eyes and leans back on the headrest, thoughts drifting to the journey ahead. If they had a non-stop run, it would be an fifteen-hour stretch to Florida. While that is achievable if he was driving alone, with the children it would be downright impossible. They will need to stop every four hours for a toilet break, and Jackie will require some time to rest as well. So his current thinking is when they reach South Carolina, they will find some back road where they can sleep undisturbed for a few hours before hitting the 1-95 again. If they stick to that schedule, they could be in Florida by 6 p.m. the next day.

213

He begins to drift off. He wonders how hot the summers get in Australia.

*

Rex shudders awake. He runs his tongue over his teeth as he opens his eyes, blinking at the view outside the windshield. He frowns. They are on a back road surrounded by barren fields, the I-95 nowhere to be seen.

"Where are you going?" he says.

"The kids need the bathroom," says Jackie, not turning to look at him.

He glances at the backseat. Both kids are dead to the world.

"They're sleeping."

"Are they," she says, flatly.

The car rocks back and forth, jolting them from side to side. Rex reaches for his gun but it isn't there. He glances over and sees it in Jackie's hand.

"What's going on?" he says.

She pulls close to a culvert and cuts the engine. Turning to look at him, she tucks a stray locket of hair behind her ear.

"I'm sorry. You seem to me to be a decent person, whatever you did, but I gotta think of my kids."

"You looked in the bag?"

"Of course I looked in the bag." She takes it from his footwell and puts it in her lap. "You know, I don't even know your name."

"Rex."

"Well, Rex. I wish you well. I hope you can turn your life around. Now please get out of the car."

He doesn't move. "You don't want to be doing this, Jackie. Trust me," he says.

"If you hadn't noticed, I've got a gun in my hand."

"You really going to shoot me in front of your kids?"

A flicker of uncertainty crosses her face.

Rex lays both of his hands flat on his thighs. "Listen, Jackie. I understand you're not a woman of means. You want the best for your kids and that's admirable, but I offered you a fair price for the journey and I intend to honor that. Now, what say you and I forget all about this little blip and get back on the road?"

She remains silent.

"Give me the gun, Jackie."

"Please do as I say," she says, lifting the gun.

Daisy's sleepy voice filters through the car. "Momma? Why are we stopping?"

Jackie goes pale. "Go back to sleep, baby."

The springs squeak as the girl sits forward. "Momma, is that a gun?" she says, gasping.

From the look on Jackie's face, it's clear to Rex that she hasn't really thought this one through.

"Sit back, baby. The gentleman's just leaving. We'll be on our way soon." But there's a waver in her voice that wasn't there before.

"Don't shoot him, Momma," says Daisy, tearfully.

Jackie softens her voice. "Oh, baby, I'm not going to shoot him. He's going to do exactly as I asked and get out of the car."

Rex says, "Tell your Momma to lower the gun."

"Don't you talk to her," snaps Jackie.

The girl starts crying. "Momma, please don't."

"Daisy, tell your mother she needs to put the gun down before someone gets hurt," says Rex, eyes still focused on Jackie.

215

"Momma, please."

"Hush baby. Everything's going to be just fine."

The girl is crying hard now and the little boy wakes up.

Jackie looks at Rex, angry. "Can't you see you're upsetting them? Get out of the goddamn car!"

Rex punches Jackie in the face. Her head flies back and blood sprays from her nose.

"Momma!" screams the girl.

Rex tries to grab the gun but Jackie scrambles for the door before he can get to it. Rex snatches a fistful of her hair and punches her again. They struggle for the gun. Jackie fights like a tiger, kicking and biting and scratching. But Rex is bigger and stronger. Suddenly, the gun goes off and a burst of red showers the windscreen and Jackie thumps face-first into the steering wheel.

Stunned, Rex stares at Jackie slumped in the driver's seat, the ear-splitting screams of the children ringing out above his head. Eventually, he reaches forward and hauls Jackie off the braying horn, exposing her bloody face and unseeing eyes.

Rex glances over his shoulder at the children. There is blood on the toddler's face.

41

I lift my eyes from the forlorn sight of Jacqueline Simons's body lying in the middle of the quiet dirt road. I study the green-blue horizon where the forest meets the sky and try and think of something nice so I don't lose it in front of everyone. I think of a swimming hole I once went to when I was a kid, and how my family and I took a picnic and lay on the warm rocks and swam all day long in the sun.

Over on the side of the grass verge, the jogger who found the body is giving a statement to Novak. Her face is red from crying. It would have been a shock to come across something like this. A pleasant late morning run had become a traumatic incident she would never forget for the rest of her life.

I take a breath and permit my eyes to sweep over Jacqueline's body again. A bullet had penetrated her right eye, leaving behind a gruesome wound. The only saving grace was at least her death would have been quick. Not like the five to eight minutes it would have taken if Rex had opted for his preferred method of strangulation. I glance at the blood, which glistens like grease in the mid-morning light. Still fresh. Whatever happened had not occurred all that long ago.

I leave the body and cross the road, stopping at the beginning of the wooded area. It's a pretty spot. Peaceful and secluded. Somewhere in the distance I hear a meandering river. While the forested area is typical of Rex's usual MO, nothing else fits. This was hurried and unplanned. Expedient. There was no pleasure in it. Then there were the children. There was no sign of them anywhere.

Novak comes over. Planting his hands on his hips, he says, "The witness didn't hear or see anything. No dust in the distance, no screams. Just found the body. That's it." He looks out across the fields. "What the hell were they doing all the way out here, anyways? And where in the hell are those kids?"

"Something happened. This isn't like him."

"I agree," says Novak.

"He's coming undone."

Novak nods. "Yeah. Coming undone with two kids in tow. Perfect. That's if he hasn't killed them already."

"We should search here," I say, looking out at the trees. "Just in case."

"Detective Tibs is on it. She's getting cadaver dogs."

I nod grimly.

Novak bends to examine the tire tracks in the soft earth. "Looks like he turned back around the same way he came in." He squints into the distance. "Got back on the I-95, maybe?"

"Highly possible." My eyes feel scratchy in the sunlight and I wish I had sunglasses.

"Where do you suppose he's headed?" says Novak. "South Carolina? Florida?"

"Difficult to say."

"If I were him, I'd ditch the car."

"That might be difficult with the children."

"Assuming they're still alive."

I stare at him.

"Sorry," he says.

"Until we know otherwise, Novak…"

"I hear you. I don't want to jinx anything."

Detective Tibs emerges from her car smiling.

"I wonder what that's about," says Novak.

42

Daisy Simons sits with her hands in her lap, not touching the fries and cheeseburger in front of her. The single thick braid trailing down the center of her back is coming loose. Wisps of brown hair have broken free from their allotted place and the elastic tie with the pretty yellow flower has slipped too far down. For a moment I wonder if Daisy has been in some sort of struggle but conclude that the slightly askew braid looks more like something she might have done herself, a few days ago maybe, possibly slept on a couple of times. I remember doing the same thing when I was a girl, self-braiding and leaving it in for longer than I should have because it took so long to do.

Daisy's watching her little brother in the adjacent playroom. He's tumbling around in the ball pit with two other toddlers. Every now and again there's a smack as one of the kids throws a ball at the Plexiglas enclosure. The girl seems remarkably composed given what she's just been through. I know it's the shock. Whatever she's experienced has not had time to penetrate all the layers of her psyche yet. No doubt it will reveal itself bit by bit over the next few days, months, and years.

I turn back to the McDonald's worker we're interviewing. Adam, a tall, thin guy who might have been twenty at a stretch.

"We noticed the kids by themselves about an hour ago," says Adam. "They'd been here for a while—the girl was sitting just the same as she is now, but holding the boy in her lap." He looks at us. "Sometimes they do that, mothers, caregivers, whatever, dump their kids here for a couple of hours and then go do shopping. Like we're a babysitting service or something."

Novak lifts an eyebrow. "Really?"

Adam sighs and shakes his head. "Happens more than you think." Adam looks over at Daisy. "Someone, Beth, I think, noticed that the little boy had blood on his face and we thought we'd better call you."

I say, "Did you see anyone drop them off?"

Adam shakes his head. "It was the morning rush. We were busy."

"What about the girl, did she speak to you or any of the staff?" says Detective Tibs.

"No, ma'am."

"Thank you, Adam," says Detective Tibs, shutting her notebook. "That'll do for now."

Adam looks at us. "Did you catch the dude yet? I heard on the radio he escaped from prison or something."

Novak winks at him. "We're working on it."

After Adam's gone, I turn to Novak and Detective Tibs. "Let me talk to Daisy on her own. I've dealt with child witnesses before and they feel more comfortable talking one-on-one."

They agree and I get to my feet and go over to Daisy, squeezing myself into the seat opposite. She glances at my belly then quickly looks away.

"Hi, Daisy, my name's Amelia."

She keeps her eyes fixed on her little brother in the playroom.

"Do you mind if I ask you a few questions?"

She shrugs.

"I hear you've been doing a good job looking after your little brother. Jedidiah, isn't it?"

"Jed," she says.

I nod. "How do you think Jed's doing?"

She frowns. "Okay, I guess."

"And what about you?"

She swallows and looks at her hands. "All right."

"Can you tell me what happened, Daisy?"

Her eyes well up. "I think my momma might be dead."

My heart aches for her. I hand her a napkin. "What can you tell me about what happened, Daisy?"

She takes the napkin and blots her eyes. "There was a fight and the gun went off. That man left her on the road." She looks at me, as if something's just occurred to her. "You could go back and check. She might still be alive."

I pause. "Daisy, I have something very hard to tell you." I put my hand over hers. "We found your mom and she was not alive."

Daisy's bottom lip trembles. "Are you sure?"

I struggle to hold back tears. "Yes."

Her face crumbles and she starts to weep. I reach out and touch her shoulder.

"I'm so sorry."

I want to hug her. She looks so small and alone.

"Daisy, I'm sorry but I need to ask you some more questions."

She lifts the sodden napkin and uses it to wipe her cheeks. "It's okay," she says, barely a whisper. "I want to help."

"Thank you, Daisy. Is there anything you can tell me about where the man was going?"

"I heard them talking about Florida."

"Okay, that's good. What else?"

"We stopped at the bus station and Momma got a bag for him."

"A bag?"

She nods. "It had lots of money in it and a gun, some clothes, too. I saw when he opened it."

I smile. "Good girl."

"I think that's what they were fighting about."

"Is there anything else, Daisy? Absolutely anything that you can tell me you think might be important?"

She extends her arm and unfurls her left hand to reveal a fifty-dollar note. "He gave me this. He said to buy some snacks for me and Jed, then he left us out there," she says, nodding toward the parking lot. "Next to the drive-thru."

"Did you see which way he went?"

"That way," she says, pointing north.

"Excellent, Daisy. Thank you."

I get up and tell Novak and Detective Tibs.

"That's Florida out of the question then," says Detective Tibs.

"That's not all. He has an escape kit. Clothes, money, most likely ID."

Novak lets out a breath. "Terrific. He could disappear into thin air."

We stand there, thinking.

"I've got an idea," I say.

I return to Daisy. Novak follows behind me.

"Daisy, did your mom have a cell phone?" I ask.

She nods. "Yes, ma'am."

"And where did she keep it? In her purse?"

Daisy nods. "Yeah."

I turn to Novak. "No purse was found with the body."

"You thinking what I'm thinking?" he says.
"It's still in the car."

43

Without taking his eyes from the road, Rex reaches for the A/C and shifts the setting to high. A rush of chilled air blasts through the vents, cooling him instantly. It feels good. Restorative. It's just what he needs. He's been clammy these past few hours. It could be a fever, from his leg. Or maybe the chaos of the last twenty-four hours is simply getting to him.

The car seems quiet now, without the children and their mother. He glances in the rearview, half-expecting to see their stunned little faces staring back it him. His eyes drift toward the dash, where he spots a bead of blood and something that could be brain matter on the rim of the odometer. It was never meant to happen. It was a tragedy for all concerned, especially those children.

He reaches for his bag, feels around, pulls out a T-shirt, and tosses it over the dash. He settles back, eyes focused on the road, hands on the steering wheel. It had run through his mind to kill the children too. Not for his sake but for theirs. What kind of life would they have now? Seeing their mother killed? Having no one to take care of them?

In the end, he'd decided against it. They deserved a chance. It was more than possible for them to go on and have a good life, even under difficult circumstances. He did it, for a while at least, before things got out of hand. But there is no reason why they would go the same way as him. The girl, Daisy, was good and kind and soft. She could go far in life with those kinds of qualities. And who knew what was possible for the little boy? He is only just getting started. So Rex left them there, outside the fast food restaurant, and wished them luck. And he meant it. He wished them all the luck in the world.

Rex reaches for his water bottle and downs a couple of Advil. His leg is killing him. That, combined with the fever, is not a good sign. He probably needs antibiotics. But there's no chance of that in the foreseeable future. His main priority now is to get out of the area as fast as he can. He'd rethought his plans after dropping the children off. Florida, or anywhere down south, is now out of the question. There is no telling what the girl heard. He'd decided to keep the car and head west to Washington, DC, and get a flight from there. Then North Dakota. Canada. Europe. He has three passports to choose from, and once he gets on that airplane he will disappear for good.

The car shudders, pulling Rex from his thoughts. It shudders again then suddenly loses all power. He looks down at the steering wheel, mystified. The car coasts along the road and Rex maneuvers it to the shoulder before it comes to a complete stop.

He tries turning the engine over but it just lets out a faltering whine. He glances at the fuel gauge. Empty. Impossible. Jackie filled it up before they left Delaware.

He reaches for the door handle, ready to check under the hood, but pauses when he catches sight of himself in the wing mirror. There's a nasty scratch running the length of his face. Jackie had gotten him good. It was so deep by the cheekbone it could have used a couple of stitches. Rex riffles through his bag, puts on a cap, pulls it down low. He gets out and opens the hood of the car. Nothing seems out of order.

226

He circles the car then crouches to look underneath. The fuel line is dripping. There's a split in the black hose. It must have happened when they went off road.

He stands looking at the highway. It's busy. Trucks and cars, a few mobile homes, the occasional motorbike. With him being a man, no one would have the good sense to pick him up—that was out of the question these days.

He looks over his shoulder. Remembers passing a gas station a while back. They might have an adjacent workshop where he could get a replacement hose. The repair is easy enough to fix himself. He grabs his bag from the car and starts walking.

44

It doesn't take long to identify the location of Jacqueline Simons's cell phone. There was no need to go through the usual arduous triangulation process, a procedure whereby network analysis software estimates the distance of a cell phone from a particular tower. Instead, Jacqueline's phone is located using its own GPS data, a much easier alternative. Not only that, the GPS is able to pinpoint the exact location of the phone—twenty miles north from where Jacqueline's body was found.

"The signal's stationary," says Detective Tibs.

My heart sinks. "You think he's dumped it?"

She blinks her frank blue eyes. "Likely."

We are talking in the McDonald's parking lot. Hardly private but the best we can do in the circumstances. My belly tightens and I feel the beginnings of a contraction. I lower myself onto the low brick fence and do my best not to show the pain on my face.

"At least we know he's heading north. That's something," says Novak.

I nod and let a breath pass through my gritted teeth. Thankfully the two of them don't notice. They are too focused on studying the map on Detective Tibs's tablet. The contraction rises then slips away. The slipping away part feels good.

"Anything else? Has he passed through toll bridges? Been pinged by a speed camera?" I ask, recovering my composure.

Detective Tibs shakes her head. "Not for now."

I stand, a little wobbly on my feet. "Let's go get this cell phone then."

The twenty-minute drive is uneventful and I'm crossing my fingers that I have seen the last of the contractions for the time being. I suspect this is wishful thinking. My belly has never been so tight and hard, the baby never so low in my pelvis. But everything's still intact and my water hasn't broken and my blood pressure's stable (apart from when I have a contraction). Those are all good things. And I'm not due for another two weeks and everybody knows first babies always come late. It's just Braxton Hicks, I tell myself, nothing to worry about.

"Is that what I think it is?" I say, squinting into the distance at the silver Mazda parked on the shoulder of the road.

Novak frowns. He checks the phone's coordinates. "It's the same location as Jacqueline's cell."

He pulls over, staying well back.

"You think he could be in there?" I ask.

"Hard to say," says Novak, staring out the windshield.

"What should we do?"

"We're in an unmarked, so we'll be safe to do a drive-by without tipping him off."

I frown. "You sure that's a such good idea? He is armed after all."

Novak looks at me. "You want me to do this one on my own?"

I shake my head. "I'm fine."

"You sure?"

"I am."

He nods pulls out onto the road.

229

"I'm not going to slow down as we get closer. I don't want to alert him so I'm just going to pass, normal-like. You take a good look as we go by. Got it?"

I swallow. "Yes."

He stares at me. "Like I say, I can do this on my own."

"Novak."

He shuts up. We get closer. My heart beats double time. We're about a hundred yards away. I can see the doors are all closed.

"I don't see anyone," I say.

"Me neither."

We drive past. I try not to be too obvious with my looking. I'm half-afraid I'll see Rex staring back at me with a gun in his hand. But the car looks empty. We stop about a quarter mile up ahead, pulling onto the shoulder. Novak stares at the rearview. I look in my wing mirror. We wait. No shadows. No movement.

"What's your gut say?" says Novak.

"He's not there."

"Agree."

Novak informs Detective Tibs, and it's not long before she and the patrol cars join us at the side of the road. The three of us approach the Mazda, the officers trailing us with their weapons drawn. But there's no cause for concern because the Mazda is empty. Novak tries the door. It's unlocked and he opens it and we look inside. I note the traces of blood on the side door, dash, and steering wheel. In the backseat, there are toys—a truck and some Lego blocks—and a fleecy blanket and booster seat. Novak reaches into the footwell in the backseat and pulls out a purse. He tips the contents onto the seat. Stray tampons. Gum. Crumpled receipts. Coins. Crumbs. Three drugstore lipsticks. Jacqueline's cell phone. We emerge and circle the exterior of the vehicle. Can't find anything wrong.

"You think he had mechanical issues?"

"Difficult to say," says Novak. "The car has seen better days, but we can't check for sure without the keys."

Novak looks across the fields. I follow his gaze and see the large industrial complex in the distance.

"What's that?"

"A canning plant. Tomatoes and corn," says one of the patrol officers.

"Big place. Lots of staff. Lots of cars to choose from," says Novak. "How far do you think that is? Half a mile? Not too far to walk. Bad leg or not."

"Or there's a small town up that way," says Detective Tibs, nodding north. "He could have gone there."

We stand there, considering.

Novak speaks. "I'd say they're our two best bets. He can't have gone far, not with his leg, and he won't want to draw attention to himself or risk being recognized. What say Amelia and I take the plant and you ask around the town, find out if anyone's seen anything?"

Tibs nods. "Agreed."

We get into our respective vehicles and Novak and I head for the canning plant, while Detective Tibs and the patrol car go in the other direction. Novak and I haven't gone far up the road when another contraction hits. I grip the armrest to stop from crying out.

"You okay?"

I turn to face the window so Novak can't see my watering eyes.

"The baby's in an uncomfortable position, that's all," I gasp.

The contraction passes and I relax back into my seat.

"Better?" says Novak.

"Yeah," I say, trying to keep my voice light. "I think she's going to work for Cirque du Soleil."

I look at my watch. That's two contractions in the last ten minutes. Strong ones, longer than usual. This is getting serious. I glance at Novak. I should tell him. But we're so close to getting Rex. I can feel it in my bones.

I spot a gas station up ahead. "Would you mind stopping?"

"Let me guess, you need to pee."

"You're smarter than you look."

He shakes his head. "You expectant mothers, just so demanding."

45

By the time he reaches the gas station, Rex doesn't feel good at all. Lightheaded and dizzy, he's having a hard time focusing. He's in a fair bit of pain, too. There's an unpleasant burn in his thigh as if someone is jabbing a hot poker into the wound. He's surprised he's deteriorated so quickly. He figures his age doesn't help, nor the lack of sleep. What's for certain though is there's no time to screw around. He needs to get to DC as quickly as possible. Once there he can find some inner-city clinic that doesn't ask too many questions and get the treatment he needed.

He squints into the late morning glare as he crosses the road. The gas station is a small affair. Two self-serve pumps. A store attached. No workshop. Rex curses under his breath. He won't be getting any replacement part here. There's a dirty white pickup at one of the pumps, but apart from that the place is quiet.

Rex hitches up the bag on his shoulder and crosses the forecourt and opens the door. Inside an old-timer with a straggly white beard stands behind the counter shooting the breeze with a man Rex suspects is the pickup owner. The old-timer gives Rex a nod and continues talking.

The radio is on. Country music. Garth Brooks or something similar. The men are discussing politics. Agreeing that things need to change. No one knows right from wrong anymore. The young'uns don't respect their elders. Not with this Twitter and YouTube and Insta-thing, showing off all the time, thinking they're stars, when they've done nothing to deserve the attention.

"Look at me," says the pickup driver, waving his hands. "I can sing like a drowned cat."

Rex heads down the aisle toward the refrigerator at the back. He opens it and feels a rush of cool air. Standing there, he lets it wash over him. His head's pounding so bad he can hardly think straight. He hates it when things don't go according to plan. Thinking on the fly means mistakes and he can't afford mistakes in his current predicament.

He grabs a carton of chocolate milk and closes the fridge, glancing up at the convex mirror. The men are still there, putting the world to rights. Rex peruses the snack aisle, lets his eyes drift over the nuts and candy bars and Cracker Jacks. Finally, he hears the bell ting as the pickup driver leaves.

Rex selects a packet of Mentos and heads for the counter. The old-timer smiles when he sees him.

His eyes drift downward and he frowns. "Say there, friend, are you okay?"

Rex follows his gaze and sees the trail of blood. He looks up. The old-timer is backing into the wall of cigarettes.

"Don't do anything stupid now," says the man, lifting up his hands.

Rex raises his gun.

46

"We need gas anyways," says Novak, pulling into the station and taking the second pump on the left.

He cuts the engine and reaches inside his pocket and pulls out three twenties.

"Get us something to eat, would you? Hot food if they've got it. Oh, and a soda. Your choice."

I grimace. "That stuff will rot your insides."

He pats his stomach. "My insides are long gone, honey."

I leave him to it and hurry across the forecourt. The baby is pressing down so hard on my bladder I'll be lucky to make it inside without an accident. I enter the store, barely glancing at the older man behind the counter, and make a beeline for the bathroom down the back. My heart sinks when I see the small square of yellowed paper taped above the handle. See attendant for key. Cursing, I quickly retrace my steps back up the aisle, my cane clapping noisily against the hardwood floor.

"I need the key to the bathroom, please," I say when I reach the counter.

The man looks in his late sixties and is wearing a *Grateful Dead* T-shirt beneath a denim shirt. There's something strange about him. I don't know what it is, the way he's standing, his deadpan expression, I'm not sure what. I wonder if I've been impolite. If, in my hurry, I sounded too demanding.

"It's all right, I'm a paying customer. We're getting gas." I glance outside where Novak is standing next to the car filling the tank. "I'm going to buy snacks, too. I'm sorry, I really need to go." I touch my stomach. "I'm pregnant."

He looks at me without smiling. "My granddaughter just had a baby two days ago. A girl. My first great-grandchild…" He drifts off.

Again, there's the strangeness I can't quite pinpoint. Like he's hyperaware of his surroundings. Alert, but trying not to show it. He pivots, stiffly, to open a drawer behind him. He rifles through, turning back a few seconds later with the key in his hand. But rather than put the key in my outstretched palm, he places it on the counter and stares at it.

"There you go," he says, swallowing.

His eyes are fixed to the cardboard tag attached to the key that says Bathroom in black permanent marker.

That's when I notice a sheen on his forehead, which is weird because the store is cool, bordering on frigid. Suddenly, I'm worried the man is having some sort of medical emergency, a heart attack or stroke or panic attack.

"Sir, are you all right? Should I call emergency services for you?"

The man's eyes widen as if I have said something frightening. Then I see it, the involuntary look to the right. So subtle I could have easily missed it. I glance down at the floor and the hairs on the back of my neck stand up on end: there's a trail of blood snaking around the corner into the next aisle. I lift my gaze and meet the man's pleading eyes. I know there's a gun on him and he doesn't want to die. Trembling now, I slowly turn my head and glance outside. Novak smiles and waves at me. I count the steps to the door. I could make it in three.

I reach for the key on the counter. "Thank you very much for the key, sir."

I pretend to turn for the bathroom but lurch for the door instead. I don't get far. Rex is upon me in an instant. I feel the weight of him on my shoulders, bearing down on me, the smell of his sweat and blood as I'm pushed to the floor. Then I'm lost somewhere beneath him unable to breathe. My baby. You're crushing my baby.

47

He stays there, on top of me, for what seems like an eternity. I am sure my baby and I will suffocate to death. All of a sudden there is light as he raises himself up and I gasp in the stale floor air.

"You're all right, you're all right," says Rex, reaching for my arm.

I scramble backward. "Get away from me," I say, still gasping.

I pat my stomach in a futile attempt to make sure the baby's okay. Mercifully, there's a kick, a small one, but a kick all the same.

"I didn't mean to hurt you, Amelia. You know I wouldn't do that on purpose."

I blink at Rex. He looks awful. His skin is pale and clammy. I glance at his leg. The fabric of his jeans is soaked in blood.

"Your leg," I say.

"I'm fine."

"No, you're not."

"Why don't you let the lady go?" says the old-timer.

The man hasn't moved from his spot behind the counter. I wonder if he's got some sort of weapon back there, secreted away. These backroad gas stations often do.

"I'm afraid we're past that now," says Rex.

That's when I see the gun in his hand. I begin to shake. I can't help it.

"Don't do this," I say.

Rex looks at me sadly. "Why did you have to come here, Amelia? You should be at home. Your lovely home. Where it's warm and safe."

"I know you were there."

He nods. "Yes."

"You could have gotten to me if you wanted."

He pauses. "I thought you deserved a chance. We all deserve a chance."

I feel the stirrings of a contraction. Not now. Oh God, not now. I do my best to keep my face passive because I don't want Rex to see.

"Let her go," says the old-timer.

Rex pivots sharply to look at him. "Shut up."

Here it comes, crawling up my lower abdominal, seizing me completely. I do everything I can not to show the agony I'm in.

"She's pregnant, for God's sake," says the old-timer.

Rex waves his gun at the man. "Don't make me say it again."

The contraction peaks then ebbs away.

I lift my shaking hand and sweep my damp fringe from my eyes. "Please, Rex, don't make it worse than it already is. Let us go."

Rex ignores me and glances out the window, keeping well out of sight. I want to look, too. Novak must be beginning to wonder where I am.

"Any other way out apart from the front door?" says Rex.

The old-timer pauses, stalling.

Rex's eyes narrow. "I asked you a question, old man."

"There's a service entrance around to the right."

"Show me."

Rex hauls me to my feet and we follow the old-timer down the last aisle.

"When's this going to end, Rex?" I say, as he drags me along. "Novak is going to know something's wrong. Was he out there before when you looked? He was gone, wasn't he? He's probably already worked it all out and is calling in reinforcements."

Rex wipes sweat from his forehead with the back of his hand. "Stop talking."

"You can end this now. You can do the right thing."

The old-timer looks over his shoulder. He lifts an arm and points to the exit. "There's your door."

Rex limps over and unlocks the bolt at the top. He opens the door a crack and looks out. He slams it shut.

"What is it?" I say. "They're here already, aren't they?"

Then the store phone starts to ring and doesn't stop.

48

"You want me to get that?" says the old-timer.

Rex points the gun at him. "Stay where you are."

Then Rex lowers himself onto the edge of a shelf filled with motor oil. He runs a knuckle across his slippery forehead and closes his eyes.

"I need to think," he says, knocking the gun to his forehead. "Why can't I think?"

"You've lost a lot of blood," I say.

The phone rings and rings. I risk a glance at the old-timer. He stares back at me silently. I feel something in my hand. The bathroom key. My mind starts ticking over.

"Answer the phone, Rex. They want to negotiate. You could ask for a medical kit."

His head snaps up. "No phone!"

I nod. "Okay, Rex, if that's what you want. What about some water? Water might make you feel better."

Rex doesn't answer. He just sits there, eyes half-focused, staring at his shoes. My belly tightens. Dread overwhelms me. Another one so soon? The contraction comes hard and fast. My knees buckle but I manage to stay upright, pressing my palm into the wall. The old-timer's eyes widen. He knows something's up, but thankfully Rex is still focused on his shoes. Breathe, breathe, breathe, I tell myself. Clamp your teeth together so you don't make a noise. In the background, the phone rings and rings. Our lifeline just out of reach. The baby is so low that I'm sure I can feel her head deep in my pelvis. How long have I got before she comes?

"Advil could help with your leg injury, friend. What about that?" says the old-timer.

I'm not sure what he's planning but I go along with it. "Yes, yes," I say, nodding. "Advil is a good idea. What do you think, Rex?"

The old-timer stars moving from his spot. "I got some over in the third aisle, I'll go get it."

Rex's head jerks up. "Stay where you are."

The old man freezes.

"He's just trying to help you, Rex. We both are."

"I don't need your…" Rex doubles over and throws up on the floor.

I jump out of the way. The old-timer begins to shout. I realize he is shouting at me.

"Go! Go! Go!"

He's right. This might be the only chance I get so I turn and run.

49

I'm closer to the bathroom than the front door so I go for that. I lumber up the aisle, terror fueling my limbs. I glance over my shoulder. Rex is on his feet at the end of the aisle, drawing his sleeve across his mouth. Oh God. Oh God. Here he comes. I urge my legs to go faster, but it's futile. I'm slow and clumsy, my useless half-foot and belly weight hindering my progress.

Even with his injury Rex is way quicker than me and it's not long before he closes in. Keep going, I tell myself. Just keep going. Ahead I see a reprieve. A rotator stand full of bargain sunglasses. I pull it to the ground and Rex tumbles over it, crashing into the floor. But he won't be down for long. Go faster, I tell myself. Just a yard more and you'll reach the bathroom door.

I can scarcely believe it when I'm holding the doorknob in my hand. I fumble with the key but can't get the thing to fit because I'm shaking so much. There's a rumble behind me as Rex gets to his knees. Hurry, goddamn it, hurry. I place one hand on top of the other and guide the key into the lock. Then I feel that familiar aching squeeze as another contraction wallops me. I double over in pain, clutching the door handle for support.

"Amelia."

Out of the corner of my eye, I see Rex standing there, pointing the gun.

"Leave me alone," I splutter.

"Don't make me do this."

I hear a noise. I look up. It's the old-timer holding a baseball bat.

"Son of a bitch," he grunts.

He swings the bat at Rex's head. There's a sickening thud and Rex crashes backward into a shelf full of beer.

"Save yourself!" shouts the old-timer.

Rex staggers to his feet and the old man swings again. Rex ducks and lifts his gun and shoots the old man in the head, killing him instantly. I stand there in shock, staring at the old man's body on the floor. Rex pivots and points the gun at me. Snapping out of it, I scramble through the bathroom door and lock it behind me. I press my forehead into the cool wood and try to collect myself. My legs are wobbling so badly I can barely stand up. Take a breath. Focus. Look around.

I turn and survey my surroundings. God. The bathroom is tiny. A lone, badly stained toilet. A dull, stainless steel basin. A faded rectangle where a mirror was once fixed to the wall. There's a small window above the sink but there's no way I'll fit. Another contraction hits. I moan and clutch my belly. The door bounces on its hinges as Rex tries to get in.

"Leave me alone," I sob.

"Open the door!"

The door bounces again. I clamber onto the sink and push open the window.

"Help!" I scream. "Novak! Help me. I'm in here!"

I can see a patch of blue sky but not much else. I push the window open as far as it will go.

"Help! Novak! Help me!"

Rex shoots the door. I scream and cover my ears. He shoots again and the door flies open and suddenly he's there, filling the frame, pulling me out, past the dead man, up the aisle, to the front of the store.

50

He pushes me down on the floor behind the counter and starts to pace. He's in a bad state. There's no telling what he might do. Above my head, the phone rings incessantly. I long to answer it and hear a friendly voice. It will be Novak. He'll have a plan to get me out. But I don't move. I dare not risk upsetting Rex any more than I already have.

I breathe through another contraction. Less than two minutes since the last one. There's no time to lose, I have to get out of here. I do an audit of my surroundings. I'm stuck on the floor behind the counter. I can't see anything from here, not the glass door, not the window. Which means Novak and the others won't be able to see me either. I'm effectively boxed in, contained in a four-by-four area, surrounded by drawers and cubby holes. It seems like the old-timer wasn't too concerned with orderliness because the cubby holes are cluttered with all manner of things. Plastic bags and newspapers and magazines and balls of string and soda cans and half-eaten candy. To the left, I spot something useful. A Stanley knife resting on top of a carton of napkins. Heart lobbing in my throat, I risk a glance at Rex. He's still pacing on the other side of the counter, muttering under his breath.

I fix my sights on the knife. It's only an arm's length away but might as well be on the other side of a canyon. Still, I have to try. I inch forward slowly, keeping a close eye on Rex. Gradually, I move across the floor until I can reach out and touch the knife.

Rex stops pacing and spins around suddenly. I pull my hand away but not before I manage to slip the knife into my pocket without him seeing.

He looks at me. "Are you all right? Are you hurt?"

I shake my head. He starts to cry. I've never seen him like this before.

"I'm not a bad person, Amelia. I wasn't going to kill him. I had to. And her, Jackie. You have to believe me."

I choose my words carefully. "Give yourself up. It's the honorable thing to do."

He looks pained. "You don't understand. I just wanted a second chance. A do-over. With the Lord's help, I was changing. I could feel myself changing. I could have done good."

"Maybe you still can."

He shakes his head sadly. "No. I don't think so. Not now."

I'm seized by an almighty contraction. It comes on so suddenly I don't have the chance to hide it. I clutch my thighs and let out a howl.

Rex crouches down, concern etched in his face. "What is it? What's happening?"

The contraction crests then fades away. Then another one, just as vicious, quickly follows. It's so bad, I see stars. I howl again.

"Is it the baby?"

I nod, gritting my teeth through the pain. There's no point in trying to hide it anymore. Oh God, the pain. The contraction merges with another. I wail loudly. I can't believe this is really happening.

"I think I'm in labor."

He looks at me, shocked. "Labor?"

"Please," I manage to gasp. "I need to get to a hospital."

"You can't be in labor. It doesn't happen just like that."

Terrible things flash through my mind. Like giving birth on this dirty gas station floor. Like Rex taking my newborn and holding her hostage.

"I've been having contractions for a while. Now they're all coming at once. You've got to let me go."

Rex stands up. "You're lying."

I shake my head. "I promise you I'm not."

I'm sobbing now, sobbing and in the worst agony I have ever been in my life. Ohhhhh. Here comes another one.

"Please, Rex, please."

I cry out again. Oh God. Oh God.

He shakes his head. "No."

He turns and limps up the aisle toward the back of the store and returns with an orange juice. He cracks open the lid and presses it to my lips. I bat it away.

"Don't. I'll be sick," I gasp.

Another contraction hits. A bad one. I moan into the crook of my arm.

"I've had complications. The baby could die."

I feel wet. I look down. A pool of fluid seeps around me. Rex sees it, too.

"It's really happening, isn't it?" he says, wide-eyed.

"Please. I'm begging you. I need to deliver her in a hospital."

He pauses and looks at me, his face suddenly clearing.

"Yes, that's it, isn't it?" he says, nodding to himself. "The key to everything."

51

He licks his dry lips and picks up the ringing phone.

"I want you to listen to something," he says into the receiver.

Rex presses the speaker button and puts the phone on the shelf opposite me. Like clockwork, another contraction hits. I look at Rex in disbelief. He can't be serious. Owww. The pain. My fists bunch and I let out a yell.

"Amelia?" Novak's voice.

"Our special mama-in-waiting is in labor, Special Agent Novak," says Rex.

"What the hell are you talking about, Hawkins? Amelia are you there?"

I can't answer, I'm too busy keening and panting.

Blinking heavily, Rex rubs his forehead. His color is really bad and he looks close to passing out.

"Here's what you're going to do, Special Agent Novak. You going to pull your car right up to the entrance. Then you're going get the hell back over there by the ridge and Amelia and I will get in the car. Then I'll drive us both out of here while you and all the other heroes out there stay put. After twenty minutes, I will call you and tell you where Amelia is. Then you can get her to a hospital and she can deliver her sweet cherub of a baby and begin her life anew."

"You know we can't do that," says Novak.

"Do as he says, Novak," I gasp.

"Amelia? I can hardly hear you. Are you all right?"

I raise my voice. "Please, Novak, do as he says. It's the only way."

"Hold on." Novak's voice muffles as he places his hand over the receiver. He comes back on the line. "Hawkins, how do we know you're not simply going to go on driving and we never see Amelia again?"

"You don't," says Rex, looking drained. "But it's all you've got."

"He's right, Novak. Oh God!" I holler as another contraction descends.

"Amelia?"

Rex takes the phone off speaker and talks into the receiver.

"So what's it going to be, Special Agent Novak? Should I start boiling the water and getting the towels ready or do we get the car?"

52

Rex lifts me up and my legs buckle beneath me. He manages to grab me before I fall, staggering a little himself. He straightens up, wheezing.

"Well, aren't we just the pair?" he says.

He is sticky and warm and smells like four days' worth of trash. The bruise on his forehead where the old-timer hit him with the baseball bat is the size of a fist and turning a nasty shade of plum. We shuffle to the door, me leaning heavily against him. I look out. There are patrol cars. An ambulance with flashing lights. I see Detective Tibs and other officers crouching behind trunks with their guns drawn. My eyes drift over their heads, to the fields beyond. The sun has gone down but a golden hue remains, casting an ominous glow across the barren landscape. Another contraction grips me. I wail. Rex squeezes my arm.

"You're all right," he says. "Hold on to me."

I bite my lip and sob, "I can't take any more."

"Just a little longer, I promise you, Amelia."

Through watering eyes, I watch Novak drive the SUV toward the shop front. He comes close, right up to the door, and stops. He stares at us through the windshield, hands white-knuckling the steering wheel. For a moment, I think he might drive right through the glass but he gets out and joins Detective Tibs behind her car.

"Ready?" says Rex.

I nod. He presses the muzzle of the gun to my head. "Just for show, okay?"

I nod again. He opens the door. There's a puff of fresh air and the smell of gasoline. We take a few steps. All guns and eyes are pointed in our direction.

"Nice and easy," says Rex, taking me around to the passenger's side of the car.

I put my hand in my pocket and reach for the knife. When Rex bends his head to open the passenger's side door, I strike, swinging my arm back and bringing the blade down hard. I go for his eyes but miss and slice open his cheek instead. The blade is so sharp, it peels back his skin like a candy wrapper. He cries out and reaches up to protect his face, dropping the gun in the process. I bring the blade back down and slice off the top of his ear.

"Amelia, stop this!" he yells.

But I don't. I swing again. I swing even though I can feel the mother of all contractions rack my body. I swing even though my knees are failing me. I swing even though I want to push this baby out right now. Rex is screaming for me to stop and I wonder if that's going to be the first thing my child will ever hear.

A green pinpoint of light appears between Rex's eyes. I frown at the dot, wondering what it is. Perhaps I am seeing things in the fading dusk. Then I get it. It's a sniper's laser. I lower the knife and step back. Rex looks at me, bewildered, blood dripping into his eyes.

"Amelia, what have you done?"

The shot rings out and a little black hole appears right between his eyes and he flies backward, slamming into the ground. His body twitches twice then goes still. I stand there, looking at him, his face in shreds and frozen in time. Someone calls my name. Novak morphs into view.

"Give me the knife," he says.

So that's what I do.

Epilogue

Ethan pushes the stroller across the grass toward the pond. We're not supposed to be on the grass, there are signs everywhere, but Ethan says he'll just flash his badge and tell them it's a police emergency if we get caught. The paved paths are too hard, he says, there are too many variables, stones and the like, disturbances that our delicate little passenger might find too jarring. The grass provides a much more cushioned experience. Superior shock absorbance, according to Ethan.

"And princess needs her shut-eye," he says, winking at me.

We've been here twice before. The first time was the second week of Sophie's life. I'd still been in a daze at that point, adjusting to the interrupted sleep patterns and breastfeeding. We stumbled upon this tiny alcove with a stone seat that overlooked a pond. Two swans had attacked our ankles.

"I think we've disturbed their love nest," Ethan had said.

He shooed them away and since then it has become our family spot, a place where we can park the stroller under the maroon maple tree in the dappled light so our baby can feel the sun on her face.

Sophie came into the world at 6:35 p.m. Seven minutes after Rex had been shot dead by a rookie patrol officer named Elvis Rodrigues. She was delivered not in a hospital but the ambulance parked on the gas station lot. After Sophie took her first breath, she mewed like a little kitten. It was the sweetest sound I had ever heard.

254

Today there are people here, sitting on our stone seat. A couple, arms intertwined, laughing at something on a mobile phone. Ethan's disappointed.

"You want to go somewhere else?" he says.

"Look. Our swans are back," I say, pointing to the pond.

Two white swans glide across the brackish water toward us.

"Don't they look beautiful?"

"I'm still thinking of the bleeding ankles."

"It wasn't that bad."

"Speak for yourself."

We make our way down to the water's edge. Ethan parks the stroller next to me, taking care to secure the brake. We watch the swans figure-eight the circumference of the pond.

I've been having the dreams again. About Rex. I haven't told Ethan. I told Lorna though. I met her in secret two weeks ago. I caught the train with Sophie to Brooklyn Park. Lorna was there already, dressed in a full-length coat, green tartan scarf wrapped around her neck, gazing out at the Hudson. The breeze was blowing through her hair and her cheeks were flushed. Seeing her out in the real world, under the natural light, made her seem more fallible and I instantly wished I had just met her in her office where I could pretend she was someone with all the right answers.

"Lorna."

She turned and smiled at me. "Amelia. It's good to see you." She looked in the stroller. "Oh, she's beautiful, just beautiful. Congratulations."

"Thanks for meeting me here. No offense, but if I have to look at that rug one more time, I'll scream."

Lorna buried her chin in her scarf and rubbed her gloved hands together. "I'll admit, it's a little unorthodox, but it makes a nice change from the office. Shall we?" she said, gesturing to a nearby park bench.

We took a seat. Out in the harbor, ferries tracked back and forth.

"So," said Lorna.

"Yeah."

"What's on your mind?"

I stifled a humorless laugh. "Oh, just about everything."

She waited for me to continue.

"I'm feeling a little lost," I said.

"Go on."

"Bereft even."

"About the baby?"

"Rex."

She paused. "I see." She pursed her lips, considering something. "Bereft is an unusual word to use in this context. Tell me more about that."

I swallowed and looked away. "I've been having dreams."

"Go on."

"About Rex."

"Rex Hawkins has been in your life for a very long time. That's not surprising."

"I hate the man."

"Do you?"

I paused. "Of course I do."

"Yet you feel bereft?"

I felt a flash of annoyance but push it aside.

"Is it normal?" I said.

Lorna leaned back on the bench. "Tell me more about these dreams."

I hesitated. "It's embarrassing."

Lorna smiled. "I hear all sorts of things in this line of work, Amelia. You'll get no judgment from me."

"It's as if I have lost a friend."

"Okay."

"A lover even," I said carefully. I felt myself blush. "I know how that must sound."

She squeezed my arm. "A dream is simply your mind's way of trying to work through a problem. Have you mentioned them to Ethan?"

"Of course not."

"Why not?"

"It's private."

"You feel shame?"

My mouth suddenly tasted like a sewer. "Wouldn't you?"

Lorna looked at me. "Rex Hawkins is a charismatic, strong-willed man. A maverick—"

I interrupted her. "A killer. A rapist..."

Lorna continued. "You were the object of his obsession for years. In a way he protected you. He was a big part of your life."

"He tried to kill me."

"Even so. With your background..."

The image of my father's swinging legs flashed in my mind.

"So what are you thinking?" I said. "Some kind of maladaptive Stockholm syndrome thing?"

"At the moment your brain is simply trying to resolve all these things, and I'm sure that eventually it will."

"And in the meantime? Rex Hawkins gets to hijack my brain? Even when he's dead?"

"It's a process, Amelia." Lorna smiled at the little bundle in the stroller. "She will help."

I exhaled. "God. When do I stop being such a mess?"

"You are not a mess," said Lorna, putting her hand over mine. "You're the bravest person I know."

That was two weeks ago. I've had three dreams since then. In the last one Rex and I were on a date in Disneyland.

"Hey, they're leaving," says Ethan, discreetly head-nodding at the couple departing the stone bench.

"When did you become so antisocial?"

"I hate people. I thought you knew that already."

Sophie gurgles in the stroller.

"Hey there, little one," I say, bending.

Sophie waves her little arms at me, eyelids fluttering across her brand-new blue eyes. I unclip the striped canvas and pull back the woolen blanket cocooning her body.

"Would you like to see the swans, Sophie?"

I pull her out and kiss the crown of her fleecy head.

"Want me to take her?" says Ethan.

"We're good."

Ethan pulls the tiny knitted beanie from his pocket and puts it on Sophie's head. After that, I hold her close. Probably too close.

THE END

More books you'll love from Deborah Rogers...

The Amelia Kellaway Series
Left for Dead
Coming for You
Speak for Me

Standalone novels
The Devil's Wire
Into Thin Air

About the Author

Deborah Rogers is a psychological thriller and suspense author. Her gripping debut psychological thriller, The Devil's Wire, received rave reviews as a "dark and twisted page turner". In addition to standalone novels like *The Devil's Wire* and *Into Thin Air*, Deborah writes the popular Amelia Kellaway series, a gritty suspense series based on New York Prosecutor, Amelia Kellaway.

Deborah has a Graduate Diploma in scriptwriting and graduated cum laude from the Hagley Writers' Institute. When she's not writing psychological thrillers and suspense books, she likes to take her chocolate Lab, Rocky, for walks on the beach and make decadent desserts.

www.deborahrogersauthor.com